MW00324612

THE
MISADVENTURES
OF THE
MYSTIFYING
NASRUDIN

TAHIR SHAH

THE
MISADVENTURES
OF THE
MYSTIFYING
NASRUDIN

TAHIR SHAH

MMXXI

Secretum Mundi Publishing Ltd
Kemp House
City Road
London
EC1V 2NX
United Kingdom

www.secretum-mundi.com
info@secretum-mundi.com

First published by Secretum Mundi Publishing Ltd, 2021
VERSION [03042021]

THE MISADVENTURES OF THE MYSTIFYING NASRUDIN

© TAHIR SHAH

Tahir Shah asserts the right to be identified as the Author of the Work
in accordance with the Copyright, Designs and Patents Act 1988.
A CIP catalogue record for this title is available from the British Library.

Visit the author's website at:

Tahirshah.com

ISBN 978-1-912383-78-8

For Peter,
With love and sincerest thanks

CONTENTS

ISTANBUL
TURKEY

Shadowman

Nasrudin went for a haircut in a side street near the Galata Tower.

Having left his suitcase just inside the door, he sat down on the chair. Within a minute or two, the barber had got down to work with his scissors. He cocked his head over to the luggage.

'So, are you travelling alone?'

'Oh no,' Nasrudin responded, 'Anwar's with me.'

'Who's Anwar… your son?'

'No, my shadow.'

The barber frowned.

'But a shadow isn't a person… so it can't have a name.'

The wise fool shrugged.

'Who says a shadow can't have a name?'

'They just don't.'

1

'Yes, they do. In my homeland all the shadows have names.'

'Really?'

'Yes.'

After lifetime of cutting hair, the barber had heard all kinds of tall tales, but never anything so strange as shadows having names.

Silence prevailed for a while.

Then, rekindling the conversation, the barber sniffed.

'So, tell me, what's the population of people in your country?'

Nasrudin narrowed his eyes.

'With or without shadows?' he asked.

SHANGHAI
CHINA

Camouflage

Although doing his best to blend in with local culture, Nasrudin managed to offend one of the most powerful Triad families in China.

Terrified out of his wits, he spent weeks hiding from the gang members.

But whenever he slipped out of his hiding place to buy food, he would spot more of them – each one dressed in baggy black clothes, every inch of their skin tattooed.

Suddenly, an idea slipped onto the stage of his mind.

He bought a black outfit, and hurried into the tattoo parlour across the street.

'What would you like tattooed?' the artist asked, taking in the unlikely customer.

Nasrudin glanced at the walls, which were covered with Triad tattoos.

He pointed to the most elaborate full-body tattoo he could see.

'That,' he said.

As he prepared his equipment and the inks, the artist cocked his head at the picture on the walls.

'If you don't mind me asking, why would a man like you want a Triad tattoo like that?'

Nasrudin smiled wryly as though he were about to outwit his pursuers.

'Camouflage,' he said.

SAN SEBASTIÁN
SPAIN

Cat Currency

Yet another financial meltdown had rocked the world's global markets, leaving Nasrudin with little confidence in established currencies.

So, he went to a butcher and spent all his money on sausages. From that day on he paid for everything in them, bartering on a system he had drawn up that was fair.

Those he met thought it was a little eccentric, but they expected nothing less from the wise fool, who had turned up in the city a month or so before. In any case, the sausages were delicious, and people were only too happy to eat them.

One night, having discovered the store of currency while its owner slept, Nasrudin's cat gobbled up his entire stock of sausages.

The wise fool was angry at the animal, but appeared as usual at the grocer's the next day.

When it was time to pay for the mountain of vegetables he had selected, the wise fool sniffed.

'I've changed currencies,' he said. 'I no longer pay in sausages.'

The grocer looked up at the customer sternly.

'Then what are you going to pay me in?'

'In a new currency.'

'And what is it?'

'It's called "the Cat".'

LONDON
ENGLAND

Reverse Alchemy

After years toiling over ancient manuscripts in the bowels of the British Museum, Nasrudin had a *Eureka!* moment.

A particular work in an ancient Sumerian scroll had been mistranslated. Although not ground-breaking in itself, the error explained why a principal alchemical spell had never worked.

Rushing back to his lodgings nearby, the wise fool gathered together the required offerings and equipment.

Then, holding a bar of lead in his right hand, he whispered the incantation – which, until then, everyone else throughout history had got wrong.

A blinding flash of light came and went.

Thrown backwards by a divine force, the wise fool grasped that the lead had been transmuted into pure gold.

Jubilant, he dared not tell anyone – not even his friends. Instead, he bought a truck-load of lead ingots, and turned every last bar into bullion.

But, boastful by nature, it wasn't long before he hinted at what had happened to his closest friend.

Within a day, everyone living near to the British Museum had heard the news, and a media sensation followed.

A week of intolerable misery came and went, at the end of which Her Majesty's Revenue and Customs sent the wise fool an estimated bill for tax on his ill-gotten gains.

Hiding in his dismal rooms, Nasrudin tried to turn all the gold back into lead. But, however hard he worked at the spell, the gold remained as gold.

'Damn it!' he exclaimed at the top of his lungs. 'You bloody Sumerians evidently didn't have to deal with the tax man!'

MUMBAI
INDIA

Brevity

is reputation as a maverick and an adventurer preceding him, Nasrudin arrived in Mumbai, the City of Dreams, where he was invited on the city's highest-rated radio show.

Despite having plenty of stories to tell, he was plagued with nerves, and found himself even more tongue-tied than usual.

Whenever the interviewer asked him anything, he answered in a single word:

'Can you describe your country?'

'Hot.'

'What kind of fruit d'you have there?'

'Melons.'

'What's the weather like?'

'Lovely.'

'I'm sure our listeners would appreciate hearing more than single-word answers,' the interviewer crooned.

'Really?' asked Nasrudin.

BAGHDAD
IRAQ

Clockwork Donkey

Nasrudin had spent all winter in his workshop, and built a clockwork donkey from scratch.

The machine contained numerous escapements, flywheels, and gears. Dragging it out on the first day of spring, he inserted the key, and wound the donkey up as though it were a clock on a mantelpiece.

Intrigued, a crowd gathered to watch.

Once the donkey was fully wound, Nasrudin slipped the key into his pocket, climbed up into the saddle, and tugged the reigns.

The donkey didn't move.

The crowd jeered.

'Perfect!' Nasrudin yelled triumphantly.

'What do you mean, "Perfect!" Your stupid clockwork donkey doesn't move!' a man at the front hissed.

'Precisely,' Nasrudin answered. 'I've spared no time or effort in making the machine the exact replica of my faithful living donkey. As everyone knows she never does what I want either!'

MEROË
SUDAN

Single Answer, Multiple Questions

lthough advised against it by his friends in the Sudanese capital, Nasrudin set off on his donkey to reach the fabled pyramids at Meroë.

The ruins were located in the desert, more than two hundred kilometres down the Nile from Khartoum. The travelling was slow and hard going, and the wise fool was soon cursing himself for imagining the journey would be easy.

Many weeks after setting out, Nasrudin crawled from the desert on his hands and knees, his donkey nowhere to be seen.

Having been spotted by a nomad close to the ruins at Meroë, he was taken into the shade of a goat-hair tent and given water.

'Don't give a thought to me!' he crowed, once he could speak. 'Please go and search for my donkey. She's stubborn, but my truest friend in all the world.'

'Where is she?' the head of the encampment asked.

'Back there, in the desert.'

Nomadic life demands that the wishes of a guest are upheld, no matter of their inconvenience to others. So, accordingly, every available man was dispatched into the desert to hunt for the donkey.

An entire week of searching passed, but the animal was not found. While the nomads scoured the desert for the donkey, Nasrudin took advantage of his hosts' hospitality – eating and sleeping better than he'd done in years.

Eventually, the search party returned to the encampment.

The headman approached the wise fool, who was picking the meat off a chicken leg.

'Respected guest,' he intoned courteously, 'where exactly did you last see your donkey?'

Nasrudin thought for a moment.

'A few miles north of Khartoum,' he said.

'But, dear friend, that's on the other side of the desert.'

The guest frowned.

'Is it really?'

'Yes.'

'How interesting.'

'Is it?'

'Yes it is,' Nasrudin declared, 'for it answers a great many questions!'

STOCKHOLM
SWEDEN

Master Reset

Nasrudin was awarded a Nobel Prize for locating a master reset switch that exists on all humans but which, until that moment, had never been known.

Pressing the switch, which was located deep in the right armpit, wiped all memory, information – and anything else – in a person's mind.

Once the award had been presented in the company of the great and the good, the wise fool was asked to explain how the reset switch worked.

Caught up with the excitement of the occasion, Nasrudin held up the index finger on his left hand.

'All you need to do,' he said, 'is to press the tip of your finger very hard, as I'm doing now, into the armpit of the right arm, and…'

'*And…?*'

The wise fool paused, blushed, and gasped:
'What am I doing here?'

DALLAS
TEXAS

God Complex

A celebrated surgeon, Nasrudin was diagnosed as suffering from 'God Complex'.

Living up to the most extreme variety of the condition, he had his hands insured for $100 million and developed a sense of superiority, the likes of which the medical world had never seen.

As time passed, he became increasingly insufferable, and was abandoned by his family and friends. The few people he continued to meet were ordered to call him 'Your Supreme Magnificence'. Believing himself to be a divine creature, Nasrudin stopped practising surgery, and shunned the company of all mortal men – whom he regarded as being well below him.

Within weeks, the wise fool was an outcast.

With nowhere else to go, he went to live in the desert. Ambling about, talking to himself, he encountered another outcast, a homeless bum.

'Hey man,' the bum asked, 'how did you hit rock bottom?'

'Please refer to me as "Your Supreme Magnificence",' Nasrudin quipped. 'And, better still, don't talk to me at all, because I'm a god.'

'That's strange,' the bum said. 'I'm a god, too.'

'Are you?'

'Yes. When I told everyone I was the true Messiah and that I had a warning, they all shunned me… and that's how I ended up here in the desert.'

'What were you warning them about?' Nasrudin asked.

The bum looked at his fellow outcast, his eyes glazing over.

'I was warning them about *you*,' he said.

LIMA
PERU

When Fraud is Not Fraud

The highlight of Nasrudin's travels through Peru was arriving at Machu Picchu as the dawn sun rose above the sacred ruins.

As he wandered through the city, he overheard a tourist moan to her husband that there were no souvenirs to buy.

An idea having been seeded in his mind, Nasrudin pulled out his pocket-knife, and cut his woollen blanket into little squares.

Arranging them on the ground near the Sun Gate, he touted the scraps of cloth as sacred Inca peace offerings.

Business was brisk.

Within twenty minutes, he'd sold them all for $10 each.

He was about to manufacture some more peace offerings, when the police pounced.

Before he knew it, he was in court, being charged with trading without a licence.

'You realize you are guilty of fraud,' the judge barked at him, 'and you could go to prison for breaking the law of Peru!'

'Oh, forgive me, Your Honour,' Nasrudin whined. 'I am a stupid foreigner who should have known better than I did.'

'Fraud is fraud,' spat the judge, 'and that's all there is to it.'

'But surely, Your Honour, it is not my fault they are so eager to believe.'

SWEETWATER
TEXAS

The Bluebottle

Nasrudin was sitting on a park bench, about to eat his sandwich, when a bluebottle with iridescent wings flew into his mouth.

Caught off-guard, he swallowed the insect.

'Damn you! Damn you!' he screeched. 'Come out at once!'

A passing homeless man asked the wise fool who he was shouting at.

'At the bloody bluebottle I've just swallowed.'

'Why don't you forget about it and eat your sandwich?'

Nasrudin looked at the homeless man indignantly.

'If I take a bite of this delicious sandwich that wretched bluebottle will get it! So, I'm holding it close to my mouth in the hope of luring it out.'

HUDDERSFIELD
ENGLAND

Right Lessons, Wrong Birds

While living in Yorkshire, Nasrudin was a well-known pigeon fancier.

Each weekend, he would spend hours teaching his birds to fly backwards. Exasperated at seeing his neighbour behaving in such a nonsensical way, the man next door peered over the garden fence.

'You're never gonna get those pigeons to fly backwards! I'll tell ya that for nowt!'

The wise fool regarded his neighbour with loathing.

'Just because they haven't yet learned to master what I'm teaching them,' he said, 'doesn't mean there's anything wrong with the lessons.'

MOBILE
ALABAMA

Fake News

Nasrudin was accused of spreading fake news on his podcast, and was reported to the authorities.

A few weeks of silence passed, and then he was called to appear in court in Alabama.

'But Your Honour, it wasn't fake news,' the wise fool protested, 'so much as simply stretching the truth.'

'Mr. Nasrudin,' the judge rejoined, glancing at his papers, 'you caused panic on an international scale! You claimed an alien invasion had taken place, and that volcanoes were erupting down the Atlantic seaboard! As you know, mass hysteria followed your claims, and untold damage has been done.'

The wise fool shrugged.

'It was nothing more than a little stretching of the truth.'

The judge glared at the accused.

'In order for stretching to take place,' he said, 'there has to be a grain of truth to stretch!'

Hoping for leniency, Nasrudin held up a hand.

'Agreed, Your Honour,' he said. 'But in this case, although existing, the grain of truth was so small I could only see it with my glasses. And on the fateful day of my podcast, I wasn't wearing my glasses – so I didn't have a way to know it wasn't there.'

TABRIZ
AZERBAIJAN

Arrogance of Ignorance

Despite being regarded by one and all as foolish, Nasrudin was stupendously arrogant.

No one could understand how a man, who apparently had no brains at all, could dare to be so conceited – more usually a preserve of intelligence.

Someone asked Nasrudin one day why he dared to be so arrogant.

He replied:

'There's a difference between an arrogant genius and an arrogant halfwit,' he mused. 'While the genius is arrogant through what he's achieved, the halfwit is arrogant by association with the genius – like the sunlight that illuminates planets in the night sky.'

BRUGES
BELGIUM

Sleepwalking

While staying in Bruges, Nasrudin clambered out of bed in the middle of the night, went out of his hotel, broke into a jeweller's shop, stole a fortune of priceless gems, and sauntered back to his hotel room… all while fast asleep.

Next morning, having studied CCTV footage, the hotel was surrounded by police. Minutes later, the wise fool had been woken up.

After he was charged, he appeared in court.

Standing in the dock, he explained how he had been asleep all night.

'Where are the gems you stole?!' the judge barked. 'Unless you reveal their whereabouts you'll be sent down for many years.'

'Gems?' Nasrudin huffed in confusion. 'I don't know what you are talking about. All I can say is that I had the most deliciously alluring dream. I had worked out how to break into a jeweller's. And, taking advantage of fact that CCTV cameras didn't cover all the route back to my hotel, I stashed the gems – all while asleep.'

The judge balked at the testimony.

'You mean to say in your dream you mounted a heist while sleepwalking?'

Nasrudin frowned.

'Actually, it was more complicated than that. You see, I dreamt I was awake, but that the version of me who was awake was daydreaming of a version of himself who was asleep, and was dreaming of a version of himself, who was in fact the version that raided the jewellery shop while asleep.'

The judge pointed a finger at the accused.

'If you think you can get off the charge by trying to confuse the court, you are sorely mistaken.'

'The last thing I'd ever wish to do would be to confuse anyone,' the wise fool answered. 'Now that I am awake, all I'm trying to do is to explain the chain of events to myself so that my dreaming mind tells my waking mind where to find the gems.'

ALBANY
NEW YORK

All in the Name

Nasrudin had heard it was easy to change one's name in America.

Although he liked his name, he was intrigued about the process. So, he went to the government building where formal petitions were filed.

The clerk in charge was the rudest man the wise fool had encountered anywhere, let alone in America.

'Fill out this form,' he barked, 'and if there's any trouble from you, I'll have you taken down to the station!'

Clutching the form, Nasrudin shuffled to a corner, filled it out, and returned to the counter.

'Read out the new name!' the clerk snapped.

Nasrudin cleared his throat.

'I'd-Be-Grateful-If-The-Damned-Clerk-Could-Show-A-Little-Common-Courtesy.'

'How dare you tell me how to behave!' the clerk blustered.

'No, no, you misunderstand me,' the wise fool said in a polite voice. 'I'm not commenting on you, sir… I'm merely following your instructions.'

'What instructions?'

'To read out my new chosen name.'

CAIRO
EGYPT

Hide-and-Seek

n a journey from Bangkok to Senegal, Nasrudin changed planes in Cairo.

The connecting flight had engine trouble, forcing him to spend a week in an airport hotel. Crazed with boredom and confined to his room, as he didn't have a visa for Egypt, he resorted to amusing himself.

First, he played noughts and crosses with himself.

Next, he played Solitaire with his playing cards.

After that, he challenged himself to a game of hide-and-seek.

No one else would have even tried to play hide-and-seek alone. But, as far as the wise fool was concerned, there was nothing unusual about it.

He hid first, while he also covered his eyes, and cried,

'Here I come, ready or not!'

After searching for himself in the bathroom, in the cupboard, and under the bed, he found himself hiding behind the curtain. Tapping himself on the shoulder, he blurted out, 'Found you!'

The next time, he hid in the shower, again, he found himself in record time.

After that, he hid under the bed.

And surprised himself, exclaiming:

'Found you for a third time!'

Both elated and irritated at the same time, the losing side of him vented his anger.

'Hey, damn it! You can't be this good at hide-and-seek!' he hollered at himself. 'You must be peeking!'

MANHATTAN
NEW YORK

Just Warming Up

 ne Sunday afternoon, Nasrudin was at his booth in Grand Central Station, reading people's fortunes.

A pretty young woman wearing a thick black veil of mourning ambled up and paid the $1 fee.

The wise fool peered into his crystal ball.

'I see travel is in the air for you,' he said earnestly.

'Of course travel's in the air! I'm at a railway station!'

Nasrudin held up a hand, indicating there was more to reveal.

'I can see this is a very sad time.'

'Of course it is!' the woman barked. 'I'm dressed in black and I'm going to a funeral upstate.'

Again, the wise fool motioned for silence, while he peered deep into the crystal.

'You're going to meet a tall, dark stranger at the funeral, fall in love, get married, have three little children who hate you, then you'll catch your husband cheating on you, turn to drink, get divorced, lose your job, and—'

'Stop!'

'Why?'

'Because it's a horrible future!'

'Bear with me madam, I'm just getting warmed up!' said Nasrudin.

GUATEMALA CITY
GUATEMALA

Mixed Up

Through using and abusing his contacts, Nasrudin was invited to perform to a packed audience on *Guatemala's Got Talent*.

He'd already toured most of Central and South America, and his routine had never failed to thrill.

When it was his turn to go on, he leapt from the wings wearing nothing but a leopard-skin leotard.

In his hand was a neatly furled flag.

Having pranced around to disco music for a minute or two, he unfurled the flag – the *Guatemalan* flag – threw it on the floor, and jumped all over it, while spitting and swearing.

Naturally, both judges and audience went berserk.

Realizing his error, Nasrudin called for calm.

'I'm so sorry!' he bellowed into the microphone. 'I've had a mix up with my props. That was my routine in Honduras, where I've just come from! Give me a minute… and I'll do it all over with the Honduran flag!'

LONDON
ENGLAND

Club of Nonsensical Rules

Nasrudin was invited to a distinguished gentlemen's club for dinner by a leading academic.

The invitation noted that there was a dress code of jacket and tie.

Down on his luck, the wise fool was flat broke. With no extra funds to spare, he couldn't afford either a jacket or a tie, and he knew no one who could lend him them.

Fortunately, he had an idea.

Taking his trousers and his shirt to a second-hand shop, he swapped them for a jacket and tie.

That evening, the wise fool turned up at the club. Although wearing a jacket and tie, he was missing his shirt and trousers.

The doorman looked him up and down.

'You look ridiculous, sir,' he said gruffly.

Nasrudin grinned.

'Thank God for that,' he responded. 'Because it seems as though I've arrived at the Club of Nonsensical Rules!'

OXFORD

ENGLAND

Comedic Constipation

Nasrudin was commissioned by a publisher to write funny stories about his life and antics.

Although he had high hopes, having sold the idea in the first place, he wasn't able to come up with anything at all.

Three months after the manuscript was due, the editor called the would-be writer.

'Where's the manuscript?' he demanded. 'We want to print it next month!'

Nasrudin winced.

'I haven't actually started it.'

'Why not?'

The wise fool sighed long and hard.

'*You* try coming up with funny stories about yourself!' he whined.

'I don't need to because I haven't sold a proposal to a publisher.'

Nasrudin slapped his hands together.

'There's only one thing worse than writer's block…'

'And what's that?' the editor asked.

'Comedic constipation!'

GREENLAND

Bear Talk

n a mission to the north of Greenland, Nasrudin strayed from the track he was supposed to be following and got terribly lost.

Having no communication with his backup team, he was losing hope.

Then, he spied a jagged lump of ice in the distance, upon which was sitting a polar bear.

With no one else to ask for help, he strode over and begged the creature for directions.

The bear looked at the explorer in disbelief.

'Don't you understand my accent?' Nasrudin asked.

'No,' the bear replied politely, 'I understood the question just fine.'

'Then why are you gaping at me like that?'

'Because I've never met a human who speaks perfect polar bear before.'

PARIS
FRANCE

Miming Full Volume

Flat broke as usual, Nasrudin was strolling through Montmartre when he saw people throwing coins to a mime, who was performing in the bright summer sun.

Taking off his jacket, he laid it on the ground, as the artiste had done, and pretended to be a mime as well.

Although he had no training as an actor, he found the work easy, and he was soon enacting a story of unrequited love.

But, unlike the mime across the street, who'd taken a small fortune in coins, Nasrudin hadn't been thrown a single cent.

Cupping both hands around his mouth, he mimed in full volume:

'Damn you… you cheapskates! I'm giving you my best material!'

MONTE CARLO
MONACO

Adulation Wanted

K nown as a high roller in the gaming world, Nasrudin had an unprecedented winning streak while gambling at the celebrated Casino de Monte Carlo.

In the establishment's long and distinguished history, no one else had ever accrued winnings on such a scale. And none had come close to the wise fool in disposing of his newly gained wealth.

As soon as he had his hands on the fortune he'd won, Nasrudin went on a spending spree to end all spending sprees.

He bought an enormous villa overlooking the sea, a private jet, a yacht, and a fleet of luxury cars. He'd hand out Rolex watches to anyone he passed, and would allow complete strangers to enjoy the fruits of his winnings.

Worrying that he was burning through his winnings too fast, an old friend cautioned Nasrudin to be careful.

'Before you know it, you'll be how you used to be – broker than broke.'

The wise fool shrugged.

'Whether I am rich or poor is of no concern to me at all,' he replied.

'How could it not be?'

'Because I'm not in it for the money.'

'Then what are you in it for?'

Nasrudin looked at his old friend, smiled vacantly, and answered:

'For the adulation.'

PAVLOVKA
RUSSIA

The Perfect Time

ollowing a complicated misunderstanding involving a box of chickens, a felt hat, and a grilled cheese sandwich, Nasrudin had become a fugitive.

Having been chased across Siberia, he'd holed up in the village of Pavlovka, east of Omsk, and was hiding in a log cabin in the woods.

It was only a matter of time before the police dogs caught his scent and tracked him down.

Flicking the switch on a megaphone, the commander called out into the darkness:

'We know you're in there!'

There was no answer, so the commander repeated his words.

'But I'm not!' came a soft voice. 'There's no one in here except for my shadow.'

The commander rolled his eyes.

'This is no time to speak such nonsense!'

'On the contrary, it's the perfect time to speak such nonsense,' Nasrudin replied. 'Because, believe me, I've got no sense left to speak!'

WATERLOO
BELGIUM

Over-prepared

Nasrudin decided to cycle around the world, starting in the Belgian town of Waterloo.

The flat landscape there would, he felt, not prove too much of a strain while he got used to a life on the open road.

Having planned the expedition for weeks, he bought himself a first-rate bicycle, panniers, camping gear, and a mass of other equipment.

Despite telling everyone he met about his plans to cycle around the world, he didn't cycle anywhere at all – not even across town.

Eventually, one of his local friends enquired gently why he hadn't gone anywhere at all.

Nasrudin shrugged.

'There was no need.'

'Why not?'

'Because all that preparation got the restlessness out of my system,' he said.

BOSTON
MASSACHUSETTS

Self-duping

Following a series of unlikely coincidences, Nasrudin was recognized as a visionary.

Overnight, almost everyone wanted to hear what he thought would happen to the world over the coming century.

Hoping to capitalize on his newfound fame, a publisher commissioned him to write a book about his prophecies. When the book was released, it sold in its millions, and the wise fool was catapulted to global stardom.

In the days and weeks after its launch, the book led to public hysteria and celebration in equal measure. Part of the reason was that the prophecies included predictions that the Earth would be invaded by blood-sucking aliens, and that geysers raining $100 bills would sprout up all over the place.

While waiting to go on a radio show in Boston, Nasrudin was asked by a technician how he could be so certain all the predictions will come true.

The wise fool shrugged.

'I've got no idea at all,' he replied.

'Then why are you making such claims?' the technician asked. 'After all, they're getting people worked up to fever pitch.'

'Because,' Nasrudin answered, 'by the time anyone finds out I'll be long gone.'

'Don't you feel guilty though, of duping people?'

Nasrudin looked at the technician hard, his eyes cold.

'My friend,' he replied, 'this is an example of people duping themselves.'

VIENNA
AUSTRIA

Out-of-Sync-Mania

However hard he tried, Nasrudin never managed to fit in.

His family and friends knew he was an oddity, and they put up with him – at least most of the time. But there came a point at which they grouped together, and suggested the wise fool go in search of treatment for his condition, which was now making their lives intolerable.

The behaviour was characterized by huge mood swings, and by living a life that was strangely out of sync. Nasrudin had taken to sleeping in the bath, bathing in the kitchen sink, and cooking meals in bed.

Packing a few belongings, he bid his friends and family farewell, and zigzagged around the world in search of someone who could cure his condition.

Eventually, he arrived in Vienna, the founding place of psychoanalysis.

A respected psychiatrist named Dr. Plank made an examination, then gave his diagnosis.

'You are suffering from a condition we call Out-of-Sync-Mania,' he said. 'The only way to be yourself again is to have a big shock.'

'You mean like when you get cured from hiccups?'

'Yes, that's right. The most effective treatment is if I frighten you when you are not expecting it.'

Nasrudin agreed, and went about life as usual.

The problem was that he was expecting Dr. Plank to frighten him, so he was always prepared – even when he was asleep.

Days passed, and the condition grew worse, as a result of expecting to be frightened.

Dr. Plank jumped out on a tram and clashed cymbals together, but the wise fool was expecting him. Then, the psychiatrist lurched at Nasrudin in a cinema.

But, again, the assault was anticipated.

Confused why the usual techniques were not working, the expert pondered long and hard.

Then he had an idea.

He phoned the wise fool.

'I would like to visit you this afternoon at 5.36 and 23 seconds.'

'Thank you doctor,' Nasrudin answered. 'You have my address.'

At precisely 5.36 and 23 seconds, the doorbell rang.

'I'm here!' the psychiatrist called out.

The wise fool opened the door.

As soon as he saw the doctor, he screamed, and his Out-of-Sync-Mania was cured.

Nasrudin was greatly impressed.

'How did you know the perfect way the scare me, doctor?'

The physician drew a hand down over his goatee.

'Because in usual circumstances an expected visitor wouldn't be the least bit scary,' he said. 'But, as you were so profoundly out of sync, I had a feeling it was the one thing that would work!'

IVANOVKA
AZERBAIJAN

Gradual Improvement

asrudin had been travelling through Central Asia for some time, and had learned a universal fact that linked all the countries in the region.

It was that there was nothing quite so important as having a reputation.

No reputation, and you were likely to be trodden underfoot.

So, before approaching the village of Ivanovka, he gathered together a group of boys and offered them a handful of coins in return for publicizing him there.

'Go to Ivanovka and tell everyone you meet that the world-famous explorer, Nasrudin, is about to arrive. Do you understand?'

Nodding, the boys took the coins, and set off across the fields to the next village.

That evening, they returned.

'You did do as I asked?'

The boys said that they had.

'And were people astonished, delighted, and amazed?' the wise fool asked urgently.

'No, no one was impressed,' said the oldest boy.

'Some jobs have to be done by a professional!' Nasrudin exclaimed.

Next morning, as the dawn broke over Azerbaijan, he dressed in his finest clothing, festooned his donkey in a strand of scarlet silk, and set off over the fields.

Riding tall, he rode into Ivanovka, his chest pushed out like a warrior returning from battle.

No one showed the least bit of interest.

'Here I am!' the wise fool yelled at the top of his lungs.

Still no interest.

'Here I am! Yes, it's me! It's Nasrudin the world-famous explorer!'

'If you're so famous why haven't we heard of you?' a homeless man begging in the main square spat.

'Well, I paid those stupid boys from the other village to tell you about me yesterday!'

The beggar hissed rudely.

'If you were really famous you wouldn't need to pay children to do your publicity.'

'That may be true,' Nasrudin retorted angrily, 'but I'm working my way up the celebrity scale gradually. How d'you expect me to become really famous until I've been moderately famous first?'

IQUITOS
PERU

The Pink-toed Tarantula

aving swallowed a bluebottle, Nasrudin had asked everyone he met what to do.

All manner of advice was given.

A dentist suggested he hang upside down in a tree and wait for the insect to fly out.

A chiropodist suggested he learn to speak the language of bluebottles and then make his case.

Then, Nasrudin's psychiatrist suggested he travel to the Upper Amazon, where a particular species of pink-toed tarantula lived… an arachnid known for its fondness for big, juicy flies.

'Just swallow the tarantula and it'll gobble the bluebottle up,' the physician said.

Never one to do things by halves, the wise fool took the expert's advice.

The next week he arrived in Iquitos, located smack bang in the middle of the jungle.

After days of adventures he reached a longhouse, in the rafters of which dozens of tarantulas were nesting.

Nasrudin lay down on the floor, opened his mouth, stuck out his tongue.

…And waited.

Three days and nights came and went.

Then, just as Nasrudin was dozing off, a plump female tarantula crept over his tongue, into his mouth, and down his throat.

Swallowing hard, the wise fool punched the air.

'That'll teach you, you damned bluebottle!' he gasped.

RIO DE JANEIRO
BRAZIL

The Secret of Success

asrudin had entered the Olympic Games as an athlete in the two hundred metres.

He may have been well below average, but quotas had to be kept up, and he was given the green light to run.

Just before the start of the race, a journalist called out to the wise fool:

'D'you think you have a chance of winning?'

'Of course I do.'

'But you're the slowest by far.'

'I have an unbeatable strategy!' Nasrudin answered cheerily.

A minute or two later, the starter's gun fired, and the race began.

Right away, two of the athletes tripped over one another and were disqualified.

Then, a hundred metres in, a third was eliminated for straying out of his lane.

And, later, two more of the runners were disqualified for having taken banned substances.

As a result, Nasrudin was given the gold medal.

At the ceremony, the same journalist who'd called out before the race did so again.

'What was your unbeatable strategy?'

The gold medal hanging around his neck, the wise fool grinned ear-to-ear.

'Simple,' he said. 'It's not about me having good fortune, but about everyone else having misfortune.'

ABERGAVENNY
WALES

The Taste of Freedom

Nasrudin was given work as a fruit-picker and, from the first moment of his employment, he did nothing but moan.

The farmer said that if he complained any more he'd be fired.

Undeterred, the wise fool made jokes about the farmer all day long. Within an hour, an informant had reported the subversion.

Nasrudin was summoned to the office.

'You can get out!' the farmer scowled, expecting the employee to beg for a second chance.

Instead, the errant fruit-picker kissed the farmer's hands.

'Thank you so much, O Great One!' he whimpered.

The farmer narrowed his eyes suspiciously.

'Don't think any amount of thanking will get me to change my mind!'

'But, O Great One… I'm not asking you to change your mind!'

'Then what are you thanking me for?'

'For freeing me from my servitude!'

MATO GROSSO
BRAZIL

Ready, Steady

After spending many weeks in deep jungle on the trail of an incredibly rare bird known as Spix's macaw, thought by many to be extinct, Nasrudin spotted one in a clearing.

His heart was pounding so hard that he almost collapsed.

Steadying his nerves, he approached the bird, with his assistant close behind.

When close to the macaw, he didn't pull out his net, as the plan had been to do.

Instead, he cupped both hands around his mouth, and hissed:

'I'll count to ten, then we're coming!'

The wise fool's assistant was both bewildered and shocked.

'So many months in this damned jungle searching for that bird, and you shout that! What are you thinking?!'

Nasrudin smiled vacantly.

'Simply giving him a head start,' he said.

CHELTENHAM
ENGLAND

The Cloak of Wisdom

The fact that Nasrudin's brain was wired differently from everyone else's meant that the wise fool was unsurpassed in cracking even the most unbreakable enemy codes.

Having been employed by numerous disreputable countries, he was poached by the British intelligence agency, MI6, and given an office of his own.

After years of service, the wise fool retired, and wrote a book about the systems he had developed for code-breaking.

The work became an instant bestseller... not because anyone could understand it, but because owning it was seen as proof of higher intellect.

The few who managed to get through the volume were feted, and regarded as geniuses in their own right.

With time, the book – which was utterly mystifying – was used by the secret services as a basis for a specialized cryptographic system of its own.

Nasrudin was asked to comment on the success of his masterpiece.

'Every great genius in human history has been a fool,' he said. 'And they recognized themselves as fools, rather than merely pretending to be wearing a cloak of wisdom.'

M'HAMID
MOROCCO

Solar Remote

The wise fool had crisscrossed the deserts of southern Morocco for weeks, travelling with nothing but a pair of she-camels, a couple of water skins, a bed roll and a little food.

Priding himself as a traveller in the mould of the great adventurers of the past, the wise fool regarded himself as the kind of man who could endure flies, thirst, and being roasted by the sun from morning until dusk.

As he tramped through the vast wasteland, certain ideas flashed onto the stage of his mind. Most of them were nonsensical but, once in a while, he had an idea that had promise.

One day, while heading to an oasis three days east of M'hamid, he had an idea that had the possibility of making his fame and fortune.

He would devise a remote control with which to modulate the sun's heat.

Ecstatic beyond words at the idea – which had the potential to change the future of humanity – he hurried to M'hamid, and then took the bus to Casablanca.

Once there, he rented a workshop in Ain Diab, and started turning his idea into reality.

Every day, he would toil from morning until night, working with all manner of technical equipment.

Weeks passed.

After returning to the drawing board a hundred times, he solved a series of mathematical problems which, in turn, allowed him to build a prototype of the device.

Although he hoped to scale it down in size, the prototype was the size of a city bus.

A local man who had befriended the wise fool, and invested in his idea, suggested that the apparatus be tested first of all outside the workshop, where it had been built.

Nasrudin shook his head.

'There's only one place to test it… the desert where I first had the idea!' he cried. 'I shall have a trailer built, and will take the machine down there, and test it *in situ*!'

And so the huge machine was transported first to M'hamid, then across the salt flats, and far beyond them to the next horizon… with the investor and a team of engineers following close behind.

Once he was standing in the exact spot at which he'd had the idea in the first place, Nasrudin gave the order for the giant remote control to be lowered onto the sand.

This was done.

The wise fool peered up at the sun, then at his watch.

Five minutes before noon.

Taking a deep breath, he turned a dial to the left, then jerked the big red lever on the side, and waited.

Nothing happened.

Then he pulled the lever up and down.

Still nothing.

'Doesn't it work?' the investor asked.

Nasrudin insisted that the machine worked, but that it would need to cool down for a few hours before they could try again.

'We will have another go at dusk,' he snapped.

At six-thirty that evening, he had a second go, just as the sun was disappearing below the horizon.

'It works!' the wise fool declared. 'My creation works!'

'The air's cooling,' said the investor, 'not because of your remote control, but because night is approaching.'

Nasrudin, who hated being caught out, glowered at his companion.

'No invention works perfectly right from the start,' he said. 'At the moment, it's working well at the beginning and the end of the day. With a little more time I'll have it working a hundred per cent.'

ST. ANDREWS
SCOTLAND

How We Play

aving been invited to play golf at St. Andrews, Nasrudin was seen picking up other player's balls, and hurling them up into the air.

Naturally, the behaviour caused an outrage.

'That's not how we play golf in Scotland!' an official shouted as he tramped across the green.

'Perhaps not,' Nasrudin answered sharply, 'but it's the way *we* play where I'm from!'

MANHATTAN
NEW YORK

Easy Questions, Please

Having swum the Rio Grande from Mexico to the United States, Nasrudin made his way to New York, where he got a job washing dishes at the Chelsea Diner.

One day, one of the waitresses offered to marry him so that he could get his green card.

The wedding took place the next day.

A week after that, immigration officials swooped on the waitress's apartment to check on the married couple. Begging them to come back next day, she got the wise fool to hurry over with a few of his clothes to make it look as though they lived together.

The investigators arrived on time and began firing questions at Nasrudin, who did his best to answer:

'What colour is your wife's toothbrush?'

'I'm not quite sure that she owns a toothbrush.'

'Where did you both meet?'

'Iceland.'

'What's her middle name?'

'Esmeralda.'

After the first three questions, the lead interrogator looked at the putative husband and frowned.

'You've failed all three questions,' he said heatedly. 'So it's quite clear to me that you're not married.'

Nasrudin let out a shrill exclamation of despair.

'Ask me where I keep my socks!' he rejoined. 'I definitely know the answer to that one!'

SOHAE LAUNCH STATION
NORTH KOREA

Mission to Mars

As a gesture of international cooperation and goodwill, the North Korean leadership invited a foreigner to be the first passenger to fly in their space rocket to Mars.

Although tens of thousands of candidates volunteered, it was Nasrudin who was selected.

Over a number of days at the Sohae Launch Station he was subjected to a series of health checks to confirm he was up to the challenge.

In the final briefing, the chief technician confirmed that the system was entirely automatic.

'All you'll have to do is lie back and enjoy the ride,' he said reassuringly.

The wise fool donned his space suit, and posed for the media.

Once the photo session was over, he took a handful of questions.

A journalist from the *New York Times* stood up.

'Astronaut Nasrudin, are you not concerned that, given North Korean technology, there's a strong chance you'll been blown to smithereens on the launchpad?'

'I have full confidence in my friends here in North Korea,' Nasrudin answered, just as he'd been ordered to do.

'What about the stress of flying the rocket ship?' called another journalist.

The wise fool gazed out at the sea of media crews, thought for a moment, and said:

'I travel to Mars all the time.'

A thousand voices called out.

'What do you mean?!' shrieked a voice at the back. 'No one's ever been to Mars!'

'*I* have,' said Nasrudin. 'Every night I close my eyes and, as I drift into sleep, I soar through the sky, into space, and reach Mars round about the time I'm ready to wake up.'

'But that's not the same thing... going to Mars in your dreams, and going there for real,' a BBC reporter spluttered.

'You're right. I'd say it's far harder to dream your way to the red planet than go there in a rocket ship.'

'How could that be so?'

'Well, in my dreams I have to imagine every last detail. In going there for real, I won't have to imagine anything at all.'

STOCKHOLM
SWEDEN

A Question of Tense

As a young man, Nasrudin was introduced to a group of Swedish students. Feeling competitive, he told them that he was one of the greatest travellers in world history.

'Where have you been?' they asked enthusiastically.

'Oh, gosh, so many places.'

'Name some of them.'

The wise fool thought for a moment or two.

'Let me think,' he said. 'I've been to my home village, and two or three others in the area. And I've been to the airport and, of course, to Stockholm, where we're sitting now. Just as I tell you, I'm one of the greatest travellers in history!'

'That's not very many places!' one of the students complained.

'I think you misunderstand me,' Nasrudin said. 'I mean to say that I *will* be one of the greatest travellers in human history – I'm simply getting my tenses mixed up.'

MOSCOW
RUSSIA

Making the Weather

fter taking a crash course in spoken Russian, Nasrudin was given a job on Russia-24 as a weather presenter.

The employment contract stipulated that his salary depended on how many messages the network received in favour of him.

On the first day, the wise fool disregarded the grim forecast and announced balmy summer weather was going to arrive at the end of the week. Even though it was freezing outside, Muscovites were buoyed by the thought of unexpectedly warm weather to come. As a result, they gave the new weatherman rave reviews.

On the second day, Nasrudin informed his audience that temperatures would soon break all records.

'You'll need sun cream and Bermuda shorts!' he clamoured.

Jubilant, the network's viewers sent messages in the thousands, praising the weatherman.

At the end of the week, the worst blizzard in living memory swept in, burying the Russian capital in five feet of snow.

As the storm howled outside, the station's chief executive ordered the weatherman to his office.

'You've made us a national laughing-stock for making the forecast up as you went along!' he bawled.

'But… but…' Nasrudin stammered.

'But, *what*?'

'But as a humble weatherman,' Nasrudin voiced, 'who was I to prevent our esteemed audience from experiencing true joy?'

DALLAS
TEXAS

The Influencer

While living in Texas, Nasrudin became well known as a social media influencer.

Whatever he said or did was followed by millions all over the world.

At first, the newly found status as an online celebrity was fantastically exciting to the wise fool.

But, with time, he grew tired of having to dream up fads for others to follow.

And before he knew it, he was slipping off track.

First, he started telling people to dress in nothing but cling film.

Then, he insisted that the only thing to eat were kiwi fruits.

Obediently, the wise fool's followers did exactly as he told them to do.

The last straw, however, came when he held up a cantaloupe melon and declared it to be a god.

Even the most diehard fans started abandoning the celebrated influencer.

'All you had to do was keep things simple,' said his friend.

'Alas,' Nasrudin replied, 'simplicity is not a word I've ever understood.'

LA REFORMA
ARGENTINA

Non-Human Language

Arriving on the Pampas with his donkey, ready to start work as a gaucho, Nasrudin was in a buoyant mood.

Since early childhood, he'd longed to soak up the macho ways of the Argentine prairies. But, from the first moment, all the other gauchos laughed at him.

They said his hat was too small, that his boots were too old, and that neither he nor his donkey had any of the qualities needed to herd cattle.

Unfazed, the wise fool climbed up on his animal and rode quietly out onto the vast grasslands.

To the amazement of the real gauchos, the cattle lined up, then followed the foreigner wherever he wanted them to go.

At the end of the day, the other cow-hands cornered Nasrudin in the stables, having been humiliated.

'What special powers do you have over the cattle?' asked one.

'How do you trick them as you do?' squealed another.

'I use no special powers or trickery at all,' he answered, 'I merely asked the cattle to do what I want them to do.'

'But cattle don't understand human language!' a third cow-hand shouted.

'Who said I was speaking *human* language?' replied Nasrudin.

VALENCIA
SPAIN

Old Tech Rules

ne Saturday afternoon, Nasrudin was found tinkering with his donkey at a friend's garage on the edge of the city.

In place of the saddle he'd put a comfortable driving seat. On either side of the creature's head he'd fitted powerful headlamps. And he'd positioned a windscreen with wipers over the animal's eyes.

Late in the day, the friend who owned the garage turned up.

'Forgive me for asking,' he said, 'instead of trying to turn one form of transport into another, why don't you just buy a car like everyone else?'

The wise fool regarded his friend pointedly.

'Because,' he explained in a firm voice, 'old technology is often better than new technology.'

'How could a donkey be better than a brand-new car?'

'Well, for a start,' Nasrudin said, 'unlike your vehicle, mine never needs new tyres, petrol, oil, or the battery charging, and she can always be trusted to find her way home.'

MANHATTAN
NEW YORK

Different Minds

asrudin had set himself up as a mind-reader in Greenwich Village and, right from the start, he did a roaring trade.

Whenever anyone sat down on the stool across from his, and paid the $5 fee, the wise fool dreamt up a long and convoluted future for them.

One day a tourist from Honduras asked for her fortune to be told. As she didn't speak any English, her nephew had agreed to translate.

The woman sat down on the stool.

Nasrudin concentrated.

'No, no,' he said regretfully. 'I can't read your future.'

'Why not?'

'Because, madam, your future is in a language I don't speak.'

SUVA
FIJI

Waves of Perfidy

His fears stoked by endless media reports of impending climate change, Nasrudin took to wearing an old-fashioned diving helmet while visiting Suva, the capital of Fiji.

Most people assumed correctly that the foreigner was an eccentric – one who'd been grossly misinformed.

'Everyone knows the seas are rising... so I don't want to be caught out!' the wise fool told a café owner in the middle of town.

'There's no doubt about that, but it's happening slowly.'

Nasrudin, who had taken to wearing the diving helmet when in bed, in the bath, and at all other times, gave the café's owner a sideways smirk.

'That's what you may think,' he said knowingly. 'But at best the sea is perfidious. After all, how can you trust anything that creeps in silently, then vanishes again down on the beach?'

MARY'S IGLOO
ALASKA

The Voice of Folly

asrudin had been hiking through the empty landscapes east of the Bering Strait when he realized that his satellite phone had run out of power.

Fearful that he'd be in grave danger were something to happen, he tried to come up with a plan to recharge the phone. Far in the distance, he spied a series of immense wind turbines swooping round and around.

Assuming they'd have a power supply, he trudged over to them.

As Nasrudin neared the turbines, the sails careening round, something deep down in his stomach goaded him to turn on his heel and flee.

At the same time, a voice whispered in his ear.

It was the voice of folly.

'Don't listen to your stupid stomach!' it cajoled. 'Climb the fence and get over to the turbines. You're sure to find a power socket there!'

So, throwing caution to the wind, he scaled the fences and hunted about for an electrical outlet.

Although couldn't see one, he did notice something that looked like a power cable halfway up the turbine's trunk.

Climbing up, he was nearing the cables, when one of the giant swooping blades scooped him up and carried him round and around.

It might have been days before he was discovered.

Fortunately for Nasrudin, a maintenance team was passing, and they saw the unlikely sight of an intruder being swept around.

Once the turbine had been stopped, and the wise fool rescued, he was ordered to give an explanation.

'It's not going to sound very plausible,' he muttered anxiously.

'Can't wait to hear it,' the team leader scowled.

'The voice of folly whispered in my ear,' he said. 'And, as it was so much more mellifluous than the voice in my stomach, I followed the voice of folly.'

'D'you expect us to believe that you're hearing voices in your head?!' the team leader yelled angrily.

'One voice was in my head, and the other was in my stomach,' Nasrudin corrected.

The maintenance chief glowered at the intruder.

'I don't believe a word of it, and am going to hand you in to the police!'

At that moment, Nasrudin's stomach gurgled very loudly.

The technician frowned.

'Excuse me?'

'It's my stomach,' Nasrudin replied.

'Oh yeah? And what's it telling you now?'

'That you're a waste of space!'

BATH
ENGLAND

Cowboy Comedian

asrudin didn't want to pay for his cracked iPhone screen to be replaced by a professional, so he ordered a new screen online and sat down to do the work himself.

Three hours after starting, his phone was in hundreds of pieces, some hardly large enough to see.

Exasperated, he scooped all the pieces up and took them to a phone repair shop on the high street.

'Thought I'd get it started for you,' he said haughtily.

The technician tipped the dismembered iPhone onto his workbench.

'Cowboy iPhone repairman, are you, as well as a comedian?'

Nasrudin scowled.

'Insult me all you like,' he replied. 'But it won't make the job awaiting you any easier.'

JULIAN
CALIFORNIA

Sharing is Caring

own on his luck following the failure of his start-up, Nasrudin was taken in by a commune of hippies.

Night after night they listened to his woes, hugged him incessantly, and reassured him that everything would all work out fine. Sharing everything they had with the wise fool, they lavished him with him food, money, and clothes.

For the first week, the wise fool lapped up the largesse, thanking Providence for his reversal of fortune. But, as one day slipped into the next, he became increasingly fraught.

Now he was back on his feet, they expected him to share as well.

After almost a month, he called the hippies around and made an announcement.

'I'm afraid I'll have to leave you all,' he said.

Stepping forward, the oldest hippie spoke for all the rest.

'We love you man!' he said tenderly. 'Is there anything we've missed in making you feel at home?'

The visitor shook his head.

'I'm having to leave because an old allergy has come back to haunt me.'

'What is it?' the leader of the commune asked.

'My allergy to sharing,' replied Nasrudin.

DEAD SEA
JORDAN

First, Examine Your Doctor

Everyone who has ever visited the Dead Sea floats in the salt-saturated waters.

Everyone, that is, except for Nasrudin.

To his surprise, and that of everyone else, he sank like a stone.

A local man suggested he get checked by his brother, who was a doctor.

A well-known hypochondriac, the wise fool turned up at the clinic and underwent an examination.

'You weigh the same amount as a battleship,' the doctor said, 'and that's why you can't float.'

Nasrudin knew he wasn't the brightest man in the world, but even to his ears the diagnosis sounded faulty.

'Can you tell me what day of the week it is, please?' he asked.

The doctor frowned for a moment.

'Blue with green spots,' he said.

'And what is the name of the French capital?'

'That's an easy one – it's Little Pink Fox.'

Thanking the physician, the wise fool got to his feet.

That afternoon, the local man who had recommended his brother passed the wise fool in the street. He asked how the consultation had gone.

'I have learned two things – one unreliable and the other certain,' he said. 'The first is that I apparently weigh the same amount as a battleship. As for the second, it's this: always examine a doctor before he examines you.'

CANDLE LAKE
SASKATCHEWAN

Freeing the Trees

Nasrudin had been recruited online as an ecological activist, and had sworn an oath to devote his life to saving the trees.

As a signed-up member of the tree-saving brigade, he'd vowed to do anything asked of him to promote the mission at hand.

The next week, he was given his orders:

First, he was to travel to Candle Lake, and get casual employment with the lumberjacks there.

Then, he was to do anything he could to ensure that the trees that had been marked for felling were spared.

Having been given a can of red paint, Nasrudin was told to go and mark every third tree, so that the team following behind with chainsaws could start the felling.

The wise fool spent all day in the forest, but failed to mark a single tree.

Instead of spraying, he was seen by another member of the crew cupping his hands to each tree trunk, and whispering at it.

'Hurry away lovely tree,' he'd call each time, 'and embrace your freedom!'

At the end of the day, he was ordered to report to the team leader.

'Why haven't you sprayed any trees, and what were you doing, whispering like that?!'

Pulling off his jacket, Nasrudin revealed himself as an activist.

His T-shirt read:

FREEING THE TREES!

The team leader guffawed.

'That's the worst plan I've ever heard of!'

'Well, it would have worked if the stupid trees did as I'd told them!' quipped Nasrudin.

MUMBAI
INDIA

The Rat

aving swallowed a pink-toed tarantula in the Upper Amazon, Nasrudin had been unable to sleep.

The thought of the arachnid dancing and prancing about in his digestive tract was unnerving to say the least. So, taking advice from an Indian godman he'd met at Lima's Jorge Chavez Airport, he decided to deal with the matter at hand.

A Google search suggested that, when it came to tarantula spiders, the best prey was a rat. And the most perfectly suited species of rat for consuming spiders was *Rattus norvegicus*, the common Indian sewer rat.

After many hours spent at 38,000 feet, the wise fool touched down at Mumbai.

No stranger to the sprawling metropolis, he made a beeline for the great sewer beneath Colaba.

A little bribery having oiled the wheels of the system, Nasrudin climbed down a bamboo ladder into the stinking underworld.

There were rats everywhere.

Thrilled to bits, the wise fool lay on his front in the sewer water, opened his mouth, and waited for a plump *Rattus norvegicus* to scurry in.

Half a moment later, a rat was inside him.

Swallowing hard, Nasrudin punched his hand in the air and exclaimed,

'Go! Go! Go Mr. Rat!'

PESHAWAR
PAKISTAN

The Pageantry of Death

A local undertaker in the so-called 'Tribal Area' was so sure Nasrudin would be shot dead for upsetting the warlords that he paid the wise fool a visit, measuring tape in hand.

'Just want to take your vital statistics,' he said obsequiously.

'What for?'

'For your coffin.'

Nasrudin balked at the idea.

'That's the last thing I'm going to blow my money on!'

The undertaker sidled up close.

'Only a fool would allow others to prepare the casket for them once they're dead,' he said. 'After all, you'll be in it for a good long while… so it makes sense to get it right.'

'But I'll be dead!' the wise fool snapped.

'That may be so, but comfort is comfort.'

Nasrudin shooed the merchant of death away, but the man wouldn't leave.

'Just imagine that you're being measured for a suit,' he lisped.

After much banter, it was agreed that a few of his measurements could be taken.

Next day, the undertaker returned with a selection of wood samples, handles, and cloth for the lining.

Again, Nasrudin protested.

But, again, he was drawn in by the mellifluous sales pitch.

By the end of the afternoon, he'd selected Package No. 9.

It included a top-of-the-range coffin. Crafted from the finest cedar, it boasted a velvet lining, exquisite veneer inlays, and solid brass handles.

'Now we have that done, will you please leave me in peace?' Nasrudin groaned.

The undertaker sighed.

'Only a fool would leave the funeral itself in the hands of others,' he said.

'What do you mean?'

'Well, these days you can't trust anyone – especially not family or friends.'

'Why not?'

'Well, leave them the money in your will, and they're likely to blow the lot on their own amusement.'

So, worn down, Nasrudin had signed up for a funeral fit for a king – with fifty drummers, professional mourners, and a troop of little children to scatter rose petals.

Coaxed to pay the full amount in advance, he requested a dress rehearsal.

'Funerals don't have dress rehearsals,' the undertaker retorted sharply.

Nasrudin looked glum.

'But how else will I be able to experience all the pageantry I've paid for?' he asked.

MOUNTAIN VIEW
CALIFORNIA

Human Sloth

asrudin was just one of thousands of people who applied for a coveted internship at the Googleplex.

But, unlike everyone else, he seemed distinctly uninterested in the prospect of working at the firm.

Another intern enquired why he was so nonchalant.

'Because I don't need Google to search for information,' he explained.

'Really? So you're telling me that you've got the sum of world knowledge in your head?'

The wise fool nodded.

'Yes, I do.'

'Then why are you trying to get an internship here?'

'So that Google put me to the test, and license me as a one-man search engine.'

'That's nuts,' the other candidate muttered.

'No, it's not,' Nasrudin answered. 'It's simply an algorithm that no one else ever thought of before.'

'And what's the secret to your algorithm?'

'Blue Matter.'

'Never heard of it.'

'Of course you haven't – I'm the only person who has.'

Unbeknown to the two prospective interns, a wall-mounted microphone had captured the conversation, and run it through a mainframe, along with all the other conversations in a thirty-mile radius.

But, unlike the others, the mention of Blue Matter caused a digital alarm to sound.

Before he knew it, Nasrudin was being escorted to a secure department, where he was asked to explain Blue Matter.

'It's the ability of any human to act as a networking algorithm in their own right, and to hold all the information in the universe in their heads.'

Pitched against Google's search engine, the wise fool managed to score full marks.

'This is incredible!' the lead engineer asserted. 'It could put us out of business.'

'That's unlikely,' replied Nasrudin.

'Why would you say that?'

'Because there's one thing built into the Blue Matter system that Google does not possess.'

'What's that?'

'Human sloth.'

BUDAPEST
HUNGARY

Enlisted Alien

Nasrudin had only been travelling through Hungary but, through an administrative mix up, he was enlisted into the army.

The next thing he knew, a pair of towering officers in uniform had turned up at his hotel and were ordering him to report for active service.

The hotel manager, a grubby one-armed man with a wall eye and a limp, sidled up to his guest.

'There's only one way to get out of military service,' he said.

'Through injury?'

The manager shook his head.

'I shot myself in the foot, poked myself in the eye, and even hacked off my own arm – and they still made me do national service.'

'So, what's the way to get out of it?'

'By being insane.'

The next week, Nasrudin reported for duty as requested. And, from day one, he did his best to act crazy. At basic training, he put gloves on his feet, shoes on his hands, painted himself blue, and ran about on all fours.

The drill sergeant demanded to know what was wrong with the conscript.

'Nothing at all!' Nasrudin cried out. 'I'm a space alien from Planet Ziwi-Pip-Pi-Poo. And in our solar system, everyone acts like I do!'

The wise fool was carted away for a psychological evaluation.

While waiting for the results at the sanatorium, he overheard one doctor telling another that he should be lobotomized.

Still pretending to be an alien from Planet Ziwi-Pip-Pi-Poo, he protested.

'You can't give me a lobotomy!' he cried.

'But it'll calm you down.'

'I don't want to be calmed down. And, besides, I don't have a human brain. You see, our alien brains contain hundreds of little glass tubes.'

The doctor looked worried.

'Well, we'd better open you up and take those out right away,' he huffed, 'because they're sure to be smashed when we send you out into battle!'

HOLLYWOOD
CALIFORNIA

Given an Inch

Nasrudin pulled strings to get a small part acting on a daytime TV soap opera.

From the moment he stepped onto the set, he started ordering everyone where to stand and what to do.

Almost instantly, the director marched over.

'How dare you try and tell me or anyone else how to do our jobs! If you don't shut up, I'll make sure you never work in Hollywood again!'

Nasrudin spewed apologies and promised to be as quiet as a mouse.

But as soon as the filming started once again, he broke his promise and gave orders.

Incensed beyond words, the director had the extra dragged to the door.

'I'm so sorry,' Nasrudin cried as he was kicked out of the studio. 'Given an inch, I can't help but take a mile.'

HERAT
AFGHANISTAN

King of the Bees

Even though he knew it wasn't right, Nasrudin suffered from delusions of grandeur.

Despite fighting them, he always felt as though he ought to have been a king or, better still, an emperor.

With no prospect of ever reaching the status he yearned for, he commissioned a carpenter to build him an imposing throne on the cheap – so at least he could play the role he imagined in his fantasies.

When the throne was ready, the wise fool strapped it to his donkey and took it back to the shack where he was staying. Furling a moth-eaten old blanket around him, he sat on the throne and watched television late into the night.

A little time passed, and Nasrudin had grandeur pangs again.

So, even though he had almost no money left, he spent it on having a crown made from painted glass, and an orb fashioned from a toilet's float.

One night soon after, the wise fool was in the local teahouse. Unable to control himself, he started boasting that he was actually a king, and that he had thousands of loyal subjects.

No one ever took Nasrudin seriously.

But his latest delusions were too much to take. So, the owner of the teahouse announced that he would be dropping by next day to meet some of the citizens the wise fool ruled over.

All night long, Nasrudin tossed and turned, fearful that he was about to be caught out. Then, as the first rays of sunlight broke over the horizon, he had an idea.

He went down into his sitting room and tried to drag the throne out into a nearby field. But it was far too heavy. So, leaving it where it was, he went out into the fields instead.

Then, one by one, he carried all the beehives he could find from the field back into his shack. Furious at having been disturbed, the bees were in a frantic mood.

As Nasrudin struggled to calm them, he heard the owner of the teahouse arriving.

Throwing the moth-eaten blanket over his shoulders, he put the crown on his head, held the orb in his hand, and sat down on the throne, irate bees swirling all around.

'Welcome!' the wise fool cried out at seeing the visitor. 'Please come in and meet my humble subjects.'

'Those are bees!' the visitor replied. 'And, what's more, they're angry bees!'

'Of course they're bees, and I am their king.'

'Well, order them to go back into the hives then… and stop stinging me!'

Nasrudin sighed.

'Alas, I wish I could,' he said. 'But time is against us. You see, in this, the Kingdom of Nasrudinia, there's a parliamentary monarchy in operation.'

'So what?'

'So, I'll have to wait for my parliament to come up with a proposal, before they debate it, and finally vote it into law.'

NEWARK AIRPORT
NEW JERSEY

Jack of All Trades

An immigration official took Nasrudin's passport at the counter and asked him what work he did back in his home country.

'I'm a plumber,' he answered.

'Plumber,' said the official, writing the word down.

'Actually,' the wise fool corrected, 'I'm an acrobat.'

The official frowned, deleted the previous profession, and added the new one.'

'No, no…' Nasrudin said again. 'I'm really a police officer.'

By this time, the official was running out of patience.

'What are you… a plumber, or an acrobat, or a police officer?'

'I'm actually a writer.'

The officer scowled across the counter.

'You'd better explain yourself or I'll have you sent back where you came from!'

Nasrudin smiled demurely.

'Well, where I'm from,' he said by way of explanation, 'the most successful men are jacks of all trades.'

JAIPUR
INDIA

Medicine for Disappointment

A grave disappointment to his father, Nasrudin was never expected to amount to anything.

Well aware that he was regarded as a failure even before he'd set out in life, he strived far harder than his brothers or sisters – so as to prove his father wrong.

As a result, he succeeded in ways his parents could only have dreamt of, and besides, he was well liked by all his friends.

Many years after his father's death, Nasrudin was reflecting one evening to his host, the Maharajah of Jaipur.

'Only now do I understand it,' he said darkly.

'Understand what?'

'That my father, a sly old fox, knew the only way to get me to reach great heights was to taunt me… to insist my life was likely to be one of consummate failure.'

The wise fool paused for a moment and stared out at the palace gardens.

'How funny that, despite his own mediocrity, he became great by making sure I reached such peaks myself.'

OMSK
RUSSIA

Pendulum Judgment

Although uncertain why, Nasrudin was hired as a judge in a suburb of Omsk.

He had no experience of being on the law-abiding side of the law before, and was thrilled at the black gown he got to wear.

As for passing judgment, he worked out a failsafe method.

Naturally, he had no interest in listening to the long testimonies. So, when the speeches and the pledging were over, Nasrudin would look at the accused, then glance at the old regulator clock on the wall and proclaim guilt or innocence.

As the weeks passed, members of the community were amazed at how the wise fool passed judgment so fast, and how he was so certain each time.

One of the other judges asked if Nasrudin ever doubted a case brought before him.

'Oh, no,' he said absently. 'They're always quite clear.'

A few more weeks passed, and the same judge grew increasingly concerned at the random nature of his colleague's judgments. It appeared that one moment he'd send an obviously innocent man down for twenty years, and let a diehard criminal go free the next.

An investigation was made.

Despite it not being his fault, but rather a matter of administrative oversight, the wise fool was charged.

By chance, he was hauled in front of a judge in the very courtroom where he had himself deliberated.

During the trial, the judge demanded to know how Nasrudin had been so slap-dash with handing out sentences.

'Oh,' the wise fool chortled. 'Well, that was the one amusing thing in a terribly dull job. I would look over at the clock on the wall at the moment I was supposed to pass sentence. If the minute hand was on the left side of the clock face, I'd say "guilty", and if it was on the right side, I'd let the accused go.'

Sitting in his chair, the judge was less than impressed.

'You have behaved atrociously and called the bar into disrepute!' he roared. 'And for that reason, I find you…'

Before the judge could finish his sentence, Nasrudin held up a hand.

'Wait! Wait! It's a minute to three!' he blustered, glancing at the clock. 'Give it another minute and I'll be innocent!'

WOOD LAKE
NEBRASKA

Shrine of the Selfless Cat

n a cross-country journey with his beloved cat, Majune, the wise fool woke up to finds his feline companion had expired.

Distraught, Nasrudin vowed to build a tomb for the animal worthy of ancient Egypt, and that he would tend the grave for the rest of his days.

Purchasing a few acres of rough ground outside Wood Lake, he set about building the mausoleum with his own two hands.

Day after day, he toiled.

And, after much exertion, the stone pyramid tomb was complete.

It wasn't long before a curious farmer turned up.

'It's a mausoleum to my darling Majune,' the wise fool explained. 'She was the kindest and most selfless of cats.'

The next week, a handful more visitors arrived, each of them having heard rumours whispered on the wind.

One by one they were told the story of the selfless cat, and in turn they marvelled at the great tomb.

The visitors kept coming.

No more than a dozen a day at first.

Then, little by little, their numbers increased.

Within three months of the cat's sad demise, a thousand people a day were turning up. Having heard the story of the selfless cat, they regarded the tomb as a place of sacred pilgrimage.

At first, Nasrudin was anxious.

After all, the people who came needed somewhere to eat, and somewhere else to sleep. They wanted fuel for their vehicles, cold drinks, tourist knick-knacks, ice cream, and so much more.

There was no longer a need to tell people of Majune, the selfless cat, as everyone had already heard the legend by the time they arrived.

So Nasrudin spent his days constructing new facilities for the pilgrims.

First, he put up a restaurant, then a motel. After that, he built a line of shops, a parking lot, and a petrol station.

As time passed, the wise fool built more and more – right there in the middle of nowhere – and the visitors came in their droves.

As the sole owner of what had become known as Selfless City, Nasrudin became very rich indeed.

Many years after the beloved cat had departed, the wise fool was sitting out on a chair, wondering about life and death.

In the distance, pilgrims were streaming into the mausoleum and using the facilities he'd built.

'Dearest Majune,' Nasrudin whispered, as he looked to the heavens, 'in life you were selfless. But, in death, your generosity knows no bounds!'

LONDON
ENGLAND

Reliability

While based in London, Nasrudin would often find himself in need of a public toilet during his long walks in the middle of the day.

A short distance behind Covent Garden, he spotted an imposing building crafted from Portland stone, and thought it would be the perfect place for the times he was in need of a loo.

Curious as to what the building was, he approached gingerly. The next thing he knew, he was welcomed inside, received with open arms, and was invited to become of a member of the brotherhood.

At his investiture into the hallowed orders of Freemasonry, the wise fool was given a sacred secret to commit to memory.

'If you divulge it to anyone,' he was informed, 'your heart will be cut from your chest, and your limbs will be severed from your body. Do you understand?'

Without a care in the world, Nasrudin nodded.

In the days that followed, the newest member of the Masonic orders blurted out the secret to everyone he met.

It wasn't long before the hierarchy of Freemasons Hall caught wind of the loose-tongued initiate.

Nasrudin was hauled in to explain himself.

'It seems to me as though we are both men on a quest,' he answered at the interrogation. 'While yours is for a reliable recruit to admit into the ranks of a secret society, mine is a little more humble.

'And, if your quest is not for the ultimate secret, what is it?'

Nasrudin blinked.

'I am merely looking for a reliable loo,' he said.

NEW ORLEANS
LOUISIANA

Faster by Donkey

Nasrudin got a job as a Deliveroo driver.

He quickly gained attention for being the only person in the organization who delivered not by car, motorcycle, or cycle – but by donkey.

More surprising still, he was continually rated the fastest deliveryman on the team.

When asked how he managed such speedy work, he replied with a single word:

'Carrots.'

'You're referring to carrots and a stick?' someone asked.

'No,' Nasrudin answered. 'I'm referring to the carrots I've used to bribe all the other donkeys with – so they don't start up in the delivery business.'

GHAN
AUSTRALIA

Wrong Way Round

While hiking in the bush near Alice Springs, Nasrudin saw a kangaroo for the first time.

Naturally, he was terrified, so began running in the opposite direction.

The kangaroo bounded after him.

Exhausted from running in the fiery heat of the Outback, the wise fool stopped in his tracks, turned, and confronted the marsupial.

'This isn't how it works!' he thundered. 'You're supposed to be frightened of me, not me frightened of you!'

NAIROBI
KENYA

On the Fence

Nasrudin was sitting in the Thorn Tree Café at the New Stanley Hotel, sipping a cup of tea, and feeling thankful for the opportunity to travel.

Noticing him sitting alone, and in the spirit of adventure for which the café was renowned, an Australian at the next table motioned for him to come over.

They chatted about their lives and their travels.

Whenever Nasrudin gave any opinion at all, the Australian shot him down – so much so that the wise fool began wishing he'd stayed at his own table.

After a silence, the Australian drained his beer, and asked:

'What are your thoughts on climate change?'

'It would be a great idea,' Nasrudin responded fitfully. 'It's far too cold in winter and too hot in summer.'

'You mean you're *for* climate change?'

Aware he was likely to be saying the wrong thing, the wise fool faltered.

'No, I'm not. Yes, I am.'

'Which… Yes or no?'

'Yesno.'

'Yesno? What kind of answer is that?' the Australian barked.

'It's the answer of a man who's sitting on a fence.'

LONDON
ENGLAND

The Gorilla Queen

Although working as a portrait painter, Nasrudin was certainly not as skilled as he might be.

The reason was that he had squandered his time on social climbing, rather than developing his technique. Although he landed commissions, he produced fabulously bad portraits.

The only thing that kept him in business was that, as he'd painted so many members of the gentry, everyone assumed he must possess some kind of skill.

One day, while Nasrudin was thinking of giving up art altogether, he received a message from the queen of a distant land. Well known for her inflated sense of ego, she was regarded as demanding in the extreme.

Even though the wise fool had tried to get out of the commission, the queen insisted, and appeared in Chelsea, at the studio he rented on Tite Street.

141

Self-possessed, vain, ugly, and ruthless in every imaginable way, the queen regarded Nasrudin with scorn.

'If your work displeases me,' she said, the words charged with loathing, 'I shall see to it that you are ruined. Do you understand?'

The wise fool nodded.

As he did so, he remembered a story he had heard as a child…

Commissioned to paint a celebrated member of the aristocracy, an artist was so fearful of her demanding nature, that he painted her right hand as a monkey's paw. When the lady viewed the portrait, her attention was focused in horror at the malformed hand. Instead of criticizing anything else, she went on and on about it.

The story gave Nasrudin an idea.

Over numerous sittings, he laboured at the portrait.

Then, months after starting, he announced that the painting, his masterwork, was at last ready to view.

No sooner had the message been sent, than the queen appeared.

The wise fool led her through into the light, where the portrait was displayed on an easel, a white sheet draped over it.

The queen reached forward and tore the sheet away.

In revulsion, she demanded to know why she'd been depicted with the head, body, and paws of gorilla – a gorilla sitting in a cage.

Nasrudin regarded his subject with irritation.

NASRUDIN'S MISADVENTURES

'You're supposed to tell me *one* thing you don't like!' hissed Nasrudin.

DAKAR
SENEGAL

Swelled Exaggeration

ne evening, at the end of a long dinner with new friends, Nasrudin described the land from which he came.

'The melons are the size of boulders,' he said, 'the streets are as clean as a hospital operating theatre, and the mountain air is so clear you can see for ten thousand miles!'

It just so happened that the waiter of the restaurant had been in Nasrudin's country, and he insisted it wasn't so marvellous at all.

The wise fool grimaced.

'It appears that you are not aware of the seventh rule of physics,' he snapped back.

'No, I'm not,' the waiter said under his breath.

Nasrudin pushed out his chest.

'Well, if you had been fortunate enough to have an education, you'd know it,' he said icily.

One of the other diners put up a hand.

'What is the seventh rule of physics?'

'The seventh rule of physics,' Nasrudin boomed, 'is that with distance travelled, exaggeration swells by three hundred percent!'

BOSTON
MASSACHUSETTS

Shaggy Dog Shipwreck

n a voyage across the Atlantic in the middle of winter, the wise fool had taken a wrong turn, and ended up on the ship's bridge.

Pulling up a chair, he started telling the captain a shaggy dog story, which went on and on for much of the night.

His concentration straying to listen to the tale, the captain failed to spot an iceberg. The next thing he knew, the vessel under his command was sinking.

By chance, both Nasrudin and the captain were saved.

At a trial that followed on dry land, the captain blamed the wise fool for telling the tale that had sucked him in as it had.

When it was his turn to take the stand, Nasrudin motioned to a police officer standing at the door of the court.

'If used in the right way, the revolver on that sergeant's belt can kill any one of us,' he said. 'If the officer aimed it at me and pulled the trigger, I would die. And if that were to happen, you would not blame the maker of the revolver, or the bullet itself. The tale I told before the shipwreck was a bullet, and I was a revolver. The loaded weapon was held in the hand of the captain who stands before you. It was he who pulled the trigger on that fateful night, and he alone.'

CHIANG MAI
THAILAND

New News

While staying in northern Thailand, the wise fool overheard an Australian tourist declare that he could eat the hottest curry on earth. Later the same day, Nasrudin happened to see the same man in a restaurant, ordering an especially spicy green curry. Hurrying over, he sat down at the next table and asked for a green curry six times hotter than the one the Australian had been served.

The waiter seemed concerned.

'Are you sure that you can eat such a curry?' he said. 'After all, you are a foreigner, and foreigners have weak stomachs.'

The wise fool swished a hand through the air. Then, in a very loud voice so that everyone could hear, he cried:

'I have a stomach of cast iron. Bring me the hottest curry your chef can make, and you'll watch me finish it all in record time!'

Ten minutes later, after much advanced gloating from Nasrudin, the green curry was set down before him. Even before he'd tasted it, he felt faint, merely from breathing in the steam.

Spoon in hand, he started to eat.

Having swallowed a single bite, he passed out, his mouth on fire.

An ambulance was called, and rushed Nasrudin to hospital, where his stomach was pumped. Next day, while checking in on the patient, the doctor said he was a fool.

'I know I'm a fool!' Nasrudin blurted. 'Now, if you thought I was clever, that really would be news!'

SEOUL
SOUTH KOREA

Humiliation

Since boyhood, Nasrudin had been a fanatical follower of Korean swordsmanship, his father having presented him with an Oriental dagger from the peninsula on his sixth birthday.

He pledged that one day, when he had saved enough money, he would travel to Korea, to learn to master the fabled two-handed sabre known as 'Ssangsudo'. Many years passed, and Nasrudin grew into a man, got married, and journeyed through life.

But he never forgot his pledge – to master the double-handed sabre.

From time to time, he would tell his wife and children about the pledge. His wife, who was never slow to needle him, cried out, 'Another one of the many things you have failed to do!'

151

Nasrudin strode into the bedroom, packed a bag, bid his family farewell, and left for Korea – right there and then.

Three weeks later, he was standing in a dojo, waiting for the first lesson to commence.

For an entire week, he was forced to sit down on the ground, then stand up, over and over, until his limbs were numb.

The next week, the master beat him with a stick, ordering the other students to make fun of the foreigner for being so pathetic.

The week after that, he was made to crawl about on his hands and knees over broken glass.

'When will we learn about the two-handed sabre?' he moaned.

Incensed that a student would dare to ask such a direct question, the master beat the wise fool with a special baton he kept in reserve for unruly pupils.

'You can pick up a sword only when you have learnt all there is to know about humiliation,' he answered. 'For humiliation is at the core of our martial art!'

Wiping the blood from his knees, Nasrudin sniffed.

'I wish I'd known that before I came all the way to Korea,' he said despondently. 'If I wanted a big dose of humiliation, I could have got it from my wife and saved on the cost of the flight.'

MANDALAY
MYANMAR

Flip a Coin

Throughout his childhood, the other children made fun of Nasrudin for many reasons, not least because he was totally inept at making decisions.

When he reached junior school, his form master gave him advice which he'd clung to ever since.

'Always keep a coin in your pocket,' the teacher had said, 'and when you can't decide between one thing and another, flip the coin.'

During his travels in Myanmar, the wise fool had – always – flipped a coin to decide where to go, where to stay, and what to eat. The coin he used was the very same one he'd had in his pocket as a boy, when the class teacher first suggested the coin-flipping approach to life. Brass, and virtually worthless, it was so worn you could no longer read the inscription on the front.

The only rule about coin-flipping was that as soon as a question with two possible outcomes flashed into his head, Nasrudin always flipped for it – whether he had a preference or not.

Having decided to walk out of Mandalay until he came to a fork in the road, he did just that. By late morning, standing at the fork, he flipped the little brass coin.

Heads.

The path on the right.

Strolling through meadows, the grass as high as his waist, the wise fool gave thanks to his good fortune and, as ever, he thanked the coin for having led to good times.

Beyond the meadow he reached another pair of paths, and he flipped the coin again.

A little later, he arrived at a village, where he found a teahouse. Taking a seat in the shade, he flipped the coin to decide whether to order a glass of orange juice or one of lemonade.

Tails.

Lemonade.

A waiter took his order, and served the most deliciously refreshing glass of lemonade the wise fool had ever tasted.

Again, Nasrudin thanked the coin for being the reason he'd experienced such joy.

Then, leaving the café behind him, he strolled through the village until he came to a river, its cool, soothing waters dazzling in the afternoon light. As he stared out at the path ahead, he saw that there were in actual fact two paths.

One in the shade, and the other in the sun.

Flipping the coin, it came up heads, which meant he had no choice but to walk in the sun.

For the next three hours, he was roasted alive as he walked down the riverbank. Mile after mile, he wished he hadn't even questioned whether to walk in the sun or the shade.

By the time he reached the next fork in the road, he was in a terribly bad mood. The same coin that had given him lemonade had led to him being so badly burnt by the sun.

Taking it out of his pocket, he glared at it menacingly.

'It's not fair that a tiny disc of shiny metal like you can bring the highs and lows you do!'

NEW XADE
BOTSWANA

The Mongoose

lthough swallowing a sewer rat had seemed like a fine idea at the time, Nasrudin soon regretted it.

From the moment the vermin was inside him, it hurried about helter-skelter, making it impossible for the wise fool to concentrate.

So, taking advice from a tourist he encountered at the Leopold Café, the wise fool decided to drop everything and travel to southern Africa.

In the grasslands there, so his informant explained, he would find *Mungos mungo*, the so-called banded mongoose – a creature that liked eating juicy sewer rats more than anything else.

Wasting no time, Nasrudin made his way to the vast hinterland of Botswana.

Once again, he lay on his stomach, stuck out his tongue… and waited.

Within a day or two, a young banded mongoose – having strayed from the pack – mistook Nasrudin's open mouth for a safe burrow, and scurried inside.

As soon as the creature was in his throat, the wise fool swallowed, leapt up, punched a fist in the air and yelled:

'Get that damned rat, and don't dilly dally!'

TAIPEI
TAIWAN

Convenient Outcome

n his travels in the Far East, Nasrudin overheard two sailors talking about a voyage they were planning to make across the Pacific on an oil tanker.

His ears having pricked up, he went over and asked whether there might be space for him on board in return for working as a deckhand.

'The captain's as hard as nails,' said one of the sailors.

'He'll work you to death,' cautioned the other.

Eager beyond words to cross the greatest ocean of all, the wise fool didn't heed the advice.

Within a day or two he was aboard the tanker, a mop in hand, and what seemed like an unending amount of deck to swab.

The captain didn't like the look of Nasrudin, and subjected him to an unrelenting onslaught of abuse from dawn to dusk.

As if that were not bad enough, he cut the wise fool's pay for complaining about the food. After that, in a bid to turn everyone else against the newcomer, he cut the rations of every man, except for the new deckhand… who was given a double ration.

Unable to take it any longer, Nasrudin called for a mutiny.

A handful of the other seamen rallied to his cry and backed him. But, before a plan could be mounted, the humble deckhand was slapped in irons.

Once on dry land, charges were levelled against the wise fool by the maritime authorities. During a hastily convened court, they demanded to know what the plan had been for the mutiny.

'I had no intention to take over the ship at all,' Nasrudin explained with a smile. 'You see, I'd heard mutterings of dissent below decks and, as a loyal member of the captain's crew, I felt duty-bound to prove for sure who was against him, our beloved master. So, I pretended to stage a rebellion, to draw the traitors out of the ranks – what in the secret services I believe they call a "mole hunt".'

'Do you expect us to believe a word of such nonsense?!' the prosecuting officer growled.

'No, not at all,' replied Nasrudin meekly, 'but it would be a convenient outcome for me if you did.'

NUR-SULTAN
KAZAKHSTAN

Inside Out

Nasrudin fell in love with Nur-Sultan and would wax lyrical for hours about the natural beauty of its mountains and forests.

Returning time and again to the city, he decided to relocate there for good. After months of jumping through administrative hoops, he got residency, and bought himself a little shack in a clearing in the forest.

One night, while sitting out on deck chairs with a friend, he gazed up at the stars and moaned how he always got lost when he drove into the city.

His friend smiled.

'Now you've settled here for good, why don't you have the city map tattooed on your chest?' he said as a joke.

The idea turned around in Nasrudin's head all night. It was a preposterous idea but, the more he considered it, tattooing the city map on his chest was the perfect solution.

So, early next morning, he went down to a tattoo studio and was the first in line when the heavily tattooed owner turned up.

'I'd like a street map of Nur-Sultan tattooed on my chest,' he said.

'What scale?'

'With as much detail as you can fit in.'

'It's going to take a long time, and will be very painful.'

Nasrudin thrust out his chest bravely.

'I'll get through it!' he exclaimed.

'Can I ask why you would ever want a street map of the city on your chest?' the artist enquired.

'Because I keep getting lost, and this way I'll never have an excuse to be lost again.'

'But how are you going to read the map?'

'What do you mean?'

'Well, if it's on your chest, you'll have to look in a mirror to see it properly.'

The artist had a point.

'Better do it back-to-front,' the wise fool said, 'and write all the words in mirror writing.'

The artist got down to work.

With the tattooing continuing hour after hour, Nasrudin whimpered and groaned, wailed, and even howled.

Without stopping once, the needle buzzed all night.

And all the following day.

Finally, after thirty-six hours of tattooing, the artist put his electric needle down.

'We're done,' he said, holding up a mirror.

Numb from excruciating pain, and utterly exhausted, Nasrudin gazed at the work of art covering his abdomen.

From that moment, he was never lost.

But, a few months after the back-to-front tattoo had been completed, the president went on television and made an announcement:

'Mirrors are objects of the Devil, and are responsible for vanity!' he declared. 'From this moment forth no one in the republic will be permitted to own a mirror! Anyone found with one – whether it be big or small – will be sent to the salt mines!'

Even before the president had finished speaking, the people of Kazakhstan started smashing their mirrors.

By the next morning, every single mirror in the country was in pieces.

Despite the lack of mirrors, everyone seemed content.

Everyone, that is, but Nasrudin.

Unable to check his road-map tattoo, he started getting lost again.

One evening, while sitting with a Kazakh friend in the usual teahouse, Nasrudin thought of the president's peculiar ruling.

'Your poor countrymen,' he said, 'having to break all those lovely mirrors.'

'And your poor foreigner,' the Kazak replied, 'having a map of the city etched into your chest you can't make sense of without a mirror.'

Nasrudin sipped his tea pensively.

'Think of it… seven years' bad luck for each one of you.'

'Well,' his friend replied, 'I'd say that having a back-to-front map tattooed on your chest is an entire life of bad luck.'

The wise fool sniffed gruffly.

'It'll all be fine,' he said.

'Why do you say that?'

'Because I've learned to dislocate my neck so I can see my chest,' said Nasrudin. 'All I need now is to learn how to turn myself inside out.'

BUQQARA
UZBEKISTAN

Discourteous

Nasrudin spotted a beautiful hoopoe, the kind he knew from his own village.

The sight of the bird brought back memories of his family and friends, and caused him to slip into a melancholic state.

Having never seen a hoopoe anywhere but in the region he was from, the wise fool assumed it had come from his home.

His mind flooded with poignant recollections, he called out for the bird to join him, and to share common memories.

Startled, the hoopoe flew away.

'Damn it!' Nasrudin snapped. 'Some birds have no manners at all! The least it could have done was to greet a stranger from its own village while travelling a distant land!'

AMMAN
JORDAN

Spaces in Between

Although modest in a rather immodest way, Nasrudin was frequently asked to give after-dinner speeches about his glittering military career.

He accepted the engagements for two reasons.

The first was that they paid very well indeed.

And the second was that they often took him to distant lands to which he'd always wanted to travel.

On one such occasion, he found himself giving a lecture in the Jordanian capital, Amman. The title of his discourse was 'How to Survive in War'.

For two hours, he regaled his audience of dignitaries with tales of close calls, ambushes, explosions, and daring-do.

After the speech, the wise fool took questions.

An impeccably dressed socialite asked how he had ever managed to survive against such terrible odds.

Nasrudin straightened his back, gave a sharp sniff, and said:

'When the bullets are flying all around, there's one – and only one – thing I keep in mind.'

'What is it?' someone called out.

'Even when the air around you is thick with enemy fire,' he said, 'there's always far more empty space than there is space taken up by bullets. My method of survival has been elementary… I simply make sure that I stay in the empty space.'

PUGLIA
ITALY

The Name of Things

An avid bee-keeper, Nasrudin impressed all the other apiarists in the area for the diligence with which he maintained the hive on the land he was farming.

Each morning, he would open its door and count as the bees departed on their quest for pollen. Then, each evening, he would again wait at the hive door, counting the tiny insects back home again.

Passing by one summer evening, a farmer – who had observed the wise fool on several occasions – was gripped with curiosity at seeing him standing at the hive, calling a name over and over.

'Roderick! Roderick! Where are you?!' he cried, his expression fearful.

'Who's Roderick?' the farmer asked.

'He's one of my flock… he hasn't returned, and I'm terribly worried.'

'Do you have names for all your bees?'

'Yes. Don't you?'

'No… of course not.'

The wise fool balked.

'But why not?'

'Because there are far too many of them to name!'

Nasrudin paused from calling out the bee's name. He pointed to the village in the distance.

'What's the name of that?' he asked.

'That's Calendano.'

'And what about that tree over there across the field? What's it called.'

The farmer strained to focus.

'Looks like an elm tree to me.'

'And what's that?' he said, motioning down to the farmer's foot.

'It's a boot.'

'If big things like villages, trees and boots can have names,' the wise fool said, 'then surely it's not too much for a few little bees to have names as well.'

VARANASI
INDIA

Off-piste

Nasrudin had never been to the holy city on the Ganges before, and was deeply moved at experiencing its rituals and life for the first time.

He spent three days down at the ghats, and exploring the maze of narrow backstreets that gave on to them.

During his stay, the wise fool bumped into a local man whom he'd met the year before in Baghdad. He suggested Nasrudin immerse himself in the Ganges with him.

Although unwilling at first, Nasrudin came round, and stripped down to his boxer shorts.

'Please remember that, as this is a holy place, certain elements of ritual must be observed,' the local said under his breath.

'Yes, yes, of course,' the wise fool answered.

Then, approaching the water, he began howling like a wolf. Hopping and howling, he splashed into the water, arms flailing from side to side.

Peeved that his acquaintance was causing a scene, the local called out:

'Why are you acting in such a strange way?!'

Nasrudin froze, rolled his eyes, and blushed.

'I'm so sorry!' he replied. 'But however hard I try, I can never help myself from going off-piste.'

MANHATTAN
NEW YORK

Perfect Ending

Nasrudin was a frustrated would-be author.

He had moved to New York months before, and was planning to write a great American novel. Despite having never finished a chapter, let alone an entire novel, he wasn't deterred.

Every week, he'd send terrible ideas to both agents and publishers, and feel affronted when – again and again – they were rejected.

One morning, Nasrudin awoke with an idea in his head unlike any of the other ideas he'd had until then. Throwing on his bathrobe and shuffling into slippers, he ran down Broadway, until he reached the offices of Random House.

He was so rattled that one of the senior editors came down to the reception to see what all the fuss was about.

'I've got it! I've got it!' Nasrudin boomed.

'Got what?' the editor enquired.

'I've got the perfect ending for the great American novel I'm going to write! It's "And then David swept out of the barn, and wished he'd never been born."'

The editor took a step back.

'What about the rest of it?'

Nasrudin let out a grunt.

'Well, now that I've got the ending,' he said, 'I'm sure your little people can fill in the rest!'

BENGHAZI
LIBYA

Box of Surprises

Nasrudin spotted a very lovely wooden box in the window of a shop.

However hard he tried to pull himself away, he couldn't stop marvelling at it – or at the label affixed to the front, which read:

A BOX OF SURPRISES

Enthralled, the wise fool slipped into the shop, and asked what was inside the box.

'It's a box of surprises,' the shopkeeper replied, 'just like it says on the label.'

'But how do I know I want to buy it until I've seen inside?'

'You don't… That's part of the surprise.'

Overwhelmed with curiosity, Nasrudin paid his money, took the box, and retreated to his hotel room.

Once inside, he ripped off the packaging and, with care, lifted up the lid.

The box was empty.

Angry at having been duped, the wise fool rushed back to the antiques shop and demanded his money be returned.

'There was no surprise in the box!' he yelled. 'You know as well as me there wasn't!'

The shopkeeper managed half a smile.

'Were you expecting it to be empty?' he asked.

'No! I thought it would have a surprise inside.'

'Did the fact you didn't find one surprise you?'

Nasrudin nodded indignantly.

'Well, that was your surprise!'

Steaming, Nasrudin tried to think of a perfect response.

'The label said *surprises* – plural! I've only had one surprise. I want at least one more!'

Losing patience, the shopkeeper reached under the counter, pulled a revolver, and pointed it at the customer.

The wise fool nearly jumped out of his skin.

'That was surprise number two… Now get out of my shop!'

NICOSIA
CYPRUS

Drastic Action

Since childhood, Nasrudin had suffered from herpetophobia – the fear of reptiles.

Although he'd managed to overcome the terror that certain species had once caused, he was more fearful of geckos than any other creature alive.

As part of his treatment, his psychiatrist insisted that he go to the Mediterranean island of Cyprus to relax.

At first everything went very well.

The wise fool toured the island, swam in the sea, and enjoyed the local cuisine.

But, as the days went by, he got a feeling of fear deep down in the marrow of his bones. It was as if he was being exposed to a gecko, even though he hadn't seen a single one of them.

Confused, he called his psychiatrist.

'I just don't know what's happening to me,' he moaned. 'There must be another reason for the pangs of fear I'm feeling.'

The doctor asked Nasrudin if he'd seen a map of the island.

'No.'

'Then I suggest you look at one, and you'll understand why I sent you there.'

Opening a map on his phone, Nasrudin zoomed out until he could see the outline of the island – the form of a gecko.

Screaming, he dropped the phone.

Then, bending down to pick it up, he shook a fist at the ground.

'You bloody gecko!' he yelled. 'I know you're trying to frighten me away! Change your shape now, or I'm going to have to take drastic action!'

VADODARA
INDIA

Nasrudin-mania

asrudin had made a wager with a farmer who tended a single field in Gujarat.

The man said the wise fool wouldn't be able dress up like a scarecrow and stand all day on the small patch of land.

Rising to the challenge, Nasrudin agreed to stand utterly motionless with outstretched arms, from dawn until dusk.

The wager stipulated that if he managed to stay in position without moving once, he'd be rewarded with a thousand rupees. But if he failed to hold the pose, he would have to pay the farmer the same amount.

Delighted at the prospect of being tested, the wise fool hurried to the field. Sitting beneath a nearby pipal tree, the farmer watched.

Hour after hour, Nasrudin stood in position, his face locked in a glowering expression so as to scare away the birds. He didn't seem to be bothered by the intense summer heat, nor by the crows pecking at the straw he had stuffed into his shirt.

Dusk came and went, and night approached.

'Alright!' the farmer called crustily at the end of the day. 'You win! I'll give you the reward.'

But Nasrudin didn't respond.

Rather, he stood there – arms out, face leering.

'C'mon!' the farmer cried out. 'It's getting late… time to go home!'

Still, the wise fool stood motionless.

Wondering if his friend was playing a joke on him, the farmer lifted Nasrudin up and carried him to the village. Despite being uprooted and taken inside, the wise fool didn't move. His arms were still outstretched, and his face was frozen as it had been since dawn.

'What shall we do with him?' the farmer asked anxiously.

'Lay him down on the kitchen floor,' his wife answered.

'I can't imagine what's got into him.'

'It must be another bout of Nasrudin-mania.'

The farmer and his wife went to bed, leaving their troubled friend on the kitchen floor.

Rising before dawn, they found the wise fool exactly as they had left him the night before – face leering and arms outstretched.

'Definitely Nasrudin-mania,' the farmer grunted over breakfast.

'What shall we do?' his wife worried.

'There's only one cure.'

'And what is that?'

'The same thing that works every time.'

Standing up, the farmer went over to Nasrudin, jabbed a hand into his armpit, and fumbled about.

'Here it is,' he said.

'Here *what* is?'

'The reset switch.'

'But people don't have reset switches. They're not mobile phones. How could he?' the farmer's wife asked in bewilderment. 'It just doesn't make sense.'

Her husband looked at her sternly, as their friend booted up.

'When did anything at all about Nasrudin make sense?' he said.

WELLINGTON
NEW ZEALAND

Rub, Shake, Bow

To his surprise, the Foreign Ministry appointed Nasrudin as ambassador to New Zealand.

Having heard good things spoken of the Antipodean nation, he was thrilled, and was quickly finding his feet in Wellington. Never one for doing hands-on research about the lands to which he travelled, he knew next to nothing about New Zealand, or its proud Maori culture.

Following the formalities of presenting his credentials, a traditional Maori ceremony of greeting was performed, at which a leader stepped forwards and rubbed his nose against that of the new ambassador.

Confused as to what was happening, Nasrudin bowed, offered his hand, and ended up hugging the dignitary.

Next day he was invited to the Japanese embassy for lunch by the ambassador.

Uncertain of the protocol, he strode forward to his counterpart, and tried to rub noses, in the same moment in which the ambassador began to bow.

The day after that, he bowed when another dignitary extended his hand.

Describing the catalogue of incidents in dispatches, he moaned:

'How can I ever be expected to master the quirks of human nature?!'

TEHRAN
IRAN

Placebo Magic

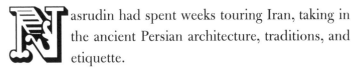 asrudin had spent weeks touring Iran, taking in the ancient Persian architecture, traditions, and etiquette.

The longer he spent in the country, the more at home he felt there. When asked why, he replied that Iranian culture was so civilized. There was a second reason, though, which the wise fool was less open in revealing to others…

The fact he was a confirmed hypochondriac.

The pharmacies were better stocked than in any other country he'd ever visited, and the price of medicine was next to nothing.

As Nasrudin reasoned it, even though doctors' charges and the medicines they prescribed were so affordable compared with other countries, there was no need to waste money on them.

One morning, the wise fool was out for a stroll with a friend when they passed a sweet shop.

'I've got to buy some medicine,' Nasrudin said. 'I'll just pop in here and stock up.'

'That's not a pharmacy,' his friend replied. 'Look at the sign... it's a sweet shop.'

Grinning, Nasrudin beckoned his friend to follow him inside.

'Those little blue ones help with my cholesterol,' he explained. 'And these pink ones are the ones I take for my asthma. Oh, and those red ones over there are what I get for my heart.'

His friend balked.

'My dear Nasrudin,' he said earnestly, 'these are sweets, and not medicine!'

'So?'

'So, you could do terrible harm to yourself!'

'That's where you're wrong,' Nasrudin answered in a low voice. 'They work perfectly so long as I don't tell the rest of my body it's being treated with the magic of placebos!'

VIENNA
AUSTRIA

Waiter Alert

While in Austria, Nasrudin was invited to meet a beautiful young woman who played in the Vienna Philharmonic.

She was evidently very cultured. Although the wise fool had meagre funds at his disposal, he invited her to one of the most expensive restaurants in town.

Fortunately, he had a plan.

The dinner went well. Nasrudin's date appeared to like him as much as he liked her, and she was evidently impressed by the cuisine, and by the restaurant itself.

Towards the end of the meal, the wise fool excused himself for a moment, and slipped into the kitchen.

Taking a pair of saucepan lids from a rack, he banged them together and shrieked:

'Fire! Fire! The restaurant is on fire!'

In the pandemonium that followed, Nasrudin led his date out of the restaurant, without having to pay the bill.

A week later, the couple returned to the same establishment, where the wise fool planned to follow the same routine as before.

Once they were done with dessert, Nasrudin slipped into the kitchen to grab a pair of saucepan lids.

But, having worked out his ruse, the waiter was expecting him.

'This is the bill for the meal you have both just consumed,' he announced, 'and this is the bill for the evening you ate last week.'

Horrified at being caught out, Nasrudin refused to pay either.

'I demand to know what kind of restaurant you're running here!' he protested. 'Last week our meal was disrupted by a fire alert, and this time it's being disrupted by a waiter alert!'

KOLKATA
INDIA

Manifestation of Irony

Nasrudin had been drawn to the city while on the trail of a magician whom he hoped to study under.

A great many visitors to Kolkata seemed to regard it with horror, but the wise fool was enthralled by the overwhelming blend of people and life. He made friends easily with the scholars, and even found himself a job tutoring the young son of an academic. The best thing of all was that the lessons were always accompanied by a hearty lunch.

One afternoon, as Nasrudin taught a class on English literature, the boy asked him to explain the word 'irony'.

Smiling wryly, the tutor held up a red chilli.

'*This* is a manifestation of irony,' he replied.

'A chilli?' the boy retorted. 'How can a chilli be anything but a chilli?'

'Because over millennia the chilli has evolved to burn the mouth of anyone who dares eat it with a ferocious, fiery taste.'

'Yes, sir, and that's why it's a chilli.'

'You are right. The chilli is a chilli. And, at the same time, it's the manifestation of irony.'

'In what way, sir?'

'Chillies are the fruit of a plant cultivated by mankind for the sole reason that it burns their mouths,' Nasrudin answered. 'Imagine if the silly chilli plant hadn't bothered trying to put us off eating it in the first place – it would have been left alone. But the fact that it burns our mouths means we've become obsessed with it.'

SOGNEFJORD
NORWAY

Questions for the Birds

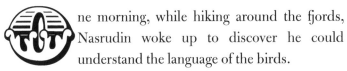ne morning, while hiking around the fjords, Nasrudin woke up to discover he could understand the language of the birds.

Thrilled at the new-found ability, he walked through the meadows, listening to the conversations other humans assumed was no more than meaningless song.

With the sun high in the air, the wise fool sat down on the grass, opened out a picnic lunch, and thanked Providence for such a magical faculty.

As he chewed on a chicken leg, a swallow tweeted from a nearby tree.

Understanding it to mean the creature wanted to peck at a crust of his bread, Nasrudin tweeted back, inviting it to join him, which it did.

Within a minute or two of conversation, the little swallow announced it was building up its strength for the long migration southwards.

'Why do you swallows have to fly such a long way?' the wise fool asked. 'It seems crazy to me.'

'If we don't migrate,' the swallow explained, 'we'll freeze to death in the winter here in Europe.'

'But why don't you just buy winter coats for yourselves?' asked Nasrudin.

KIEV

UKRAINE

Random Sameness

With all his funds used up, Nasrudin had been forced to sleep on a bench at the Pasazhyrskyi Railway Station.

After a freezing and uncomfortable night, he went to the public toilets and washed his face. He was about to leave when he overheard two men speaking in one of the stalls.

'There's an immense treasure buried in the Holosiivskyi Forest,' said the first. 'It's bullion buried in the war.'

'D'you know exactly where it is?' asked the second.

'Yes, I've got a map.'

'Let's go right away and dig it up.'

'Better wait until the snow thaws.'

Tiptoeing out of the toilets, Nasrudin got his hands on a spade and made his way to the Holosiivskyi Forest.

By lunchtime, he was digging randomly.

With the ground rock-solid, it was a thankless task. But undeterred, he continued to dig all day.

Then all the next day.

And all the next week.

Needless to say, he didn't find any treasure. Even more down on his luck than usual, he returned to the railway station where he'd overheard the two would-be treasure-seekers.

Filthy after days of digging, the wise fool slipped into the public toilets and washed himself.

To his surprise, and his delight, he heard the same two voices as before, conspiring in one of the stalls.

Unable to help himself, Nasrudin went over, and explained how he'd been digging for days on end, had found nothing, and didn't believe there was a treasure.

At first, the men were furious that their private conversation had been overheard.

But, once they calmed down, one of them asked:

'How could you have hoped to find the treasure if you didn't know the right coordinates?'

Nasrudin shrugged.

'Well, the forest all looked the same to me,' he said.

'So, that's why you need to know the coordinates.'

Again, Nasrudin shrugged.

'Well as it's all the same,' he said, 'it surely stands to reason that digging anywhere will do.'

THE BRONX
NEW YORK

Knowing Who Counts

asrudin hadn't been in the United States very long when he bumped into an old friend who persuaded him to become an Uber driver.

The next thing the wise fool knew, he was driving night shifts. But, unlike most of the other drivers on the city's streets, he was awfully substandard.

First, he had trouble finding the customers. Then, when he had actually managed to connect, he bored them senseless with interminable stories of his adventures. When not recounting tall tales, he was moaning about the low wages, or complaining about the firm's management. As for his driving, it was dangerous at best – each journey a white-knuckle ride of near misses.

Yet, when it came to the annual Uber Awards, Nasrudin won the coveted Best Driver Prize.

The friend who had coaxed him to drive in the first place couldn't understand how Nasrudin had won the prestigious award – presented by a board of special judges.

Asked whether it was a mistake, the wise fool grinned ear-to-ear.

'I may not be a good driver,' he answered. 'But, unlike the rest of them, I know what counts.'

'So, what is it that counts?'

'Not trying to impress the customers, but rather the judges.'

CARDIFF
WALES

Eyes for Optimism

asrudin won a prize for being the most optimistic person in the world, and travelled to Cardiff to collect it.

In his acceptance speech he explained how, as the world's most optimistic man, he was always optimistic – even when there was absolutely no hope.

The day after the ceremony, he was walking down the street with the massive trophy. And, not being able to see over it, he tripped and fell.

The next thing he knew, he was lying in a hospital bed, encased from head to toe in plaster.

One of the nurses checked if he was still optimistic.

'Yes!' he exclaimed. 'Because I get to spend the next six months lying on my back watching television, looking out at the trees, and listening to the birdsong.'

The nurse winced.

'But you've broken your back in twenty places! How can you be so eternally optimistic?'

Nasrudin thought for a moment.

'Because optimism is light and pessimism is darkness,' he said. 'I was born with eyes, which means I'm supposed to live in the light.'

DALSLAND
SWEDEN

Cloud Maps 2.0

Nasrudin was lost in one of the great forests of Dalsland in southern Sweden.

For hours he'd been going in circles and, the summer sun dazzling overhead, he was losing hope.

Exhausted, he leant back and stared up at the sky.

'O Great Creator!' he called. 'Can't you send me a map so that I can get back to the cottage?'

Frowning, his gaze focused on the cloud formations high in the atmosphere. To his surprise and joy, he realized that the clouds appeared to be a map of the forest in which he was lost.

Giving thanks, he followed the map and was soon back at the cottage where he was staying.

Over the coming days, the wise fool told everyone about his miraculous feat of celestial navigation. Some scoffed, but a few took it seriously.

Buoyed by enthusiasm for his story, Nasrudin developed an entire field of science which he styled as 'Cloud Maps'.

A local TV channel asked him to explain the thinking behind Cloud Maps to its viewers. First, Nasrudin retold the background, of how he'd got lost in the forest and was saved by the map in the sky.

'The great thing about Cloud Maps,' he said enthusiastically, 'is that they're always there – above you. You don't have to carry a map in your pocket, or even remember your reading glasses.'

The interviewer appeared to be confused.

'I don't get it,' she said.

'Don't get *what*?'

'Well, what if the exact map you need isn't right above you when you need it?'

'Of course that does happen from time to time,' Nasrudin answered. 'And it's the reason I'm working on Cloud Maps 2.0.'

CAIRNS
AUSTRALIA

Blue-Ringed Octopus

espite high hopes that his troubles would be over – having swallowed the banded mongoose in Botswana – Nasrudin had a dreadful stomach ache.

So, following the advice of a passing rancher from Queenland, he travelled by land and sea to Cairns in northern Australia.

In its waters, he was informed, the fabled blue-ringed octopus lived – a creature perfectly suited to devouring mongooses from the African savannah.

Not naturally comfortable in shark-infested waters, the wise fool paddled out onto the reef, opened his mouth wide, and waited.

After swallowing a couple of sea urchins, stray fish, and at least one lump of razor-sharp coral, a female blue-ringed octopus swam out from the shadows and into Nasrudin's mouth.

Gurgling, he danced a jig underwater, punched the air, and gave thanks to Providence, for saving him from the trials and tribulations caused long before by the humble bluebottle.

CAMBRIDGE
MASSACHUSETTS

Dropping Out

After a frenzy of networking, Nasrudin was offered an interview at Harvard University.

None of his friends could understand why he had spent quite so much time in getting considered as an applicant, for there was no way he could ever have been described as being academic.

The first question at the interview was why he wanted to join the university.

Having given the question appropriate consideration, he looked at the interviewer in the eye and replied in little more than a whisper:

'I want to study at Harvard because here in America all the most successful people seem to have dropped out of fine institutions such as this. Don't tell anyone else, but my plan's to drop out as soon as I've been accepted – just like all the best people do.'

DARRA
PAKISTAN

Guns Not Bullets

Although Nasrudin disliked weapons, he was accompanying a gun-crazed friend through the town of Darra, at the edge of the so-called Tribal Area.

The community was famous throughout Central Asia for copying everything from pen-guns to rocket-propelled grenades.

'If I had my way,' his friend roared, 'every man, woman, and child would be forced to own guns!'

'I have no problem with that,' Nasrudin replied. 'So long as none of them owned any bullets.'

WESTERN DESERT
EGYPT

Danger Warning

Nasrudin was trekking through the Western Desert when he came upon a First Kingdom temple in the middle of nowhere.

Awed by what had once been hallowed ground, he took off his shoes and went inside.

On entering, he heard voices.

Assuming he was witnessing oracles speaking to each other, he listened.

'As usual, we'll rob the next man who turns up,' said the first.

'Then, we'll slit his throat,' said the second.

'After that, we will bury his body with all the others at the back of the temple.'

Tiptoeing out, the wise fool made his way back to his donkey.

'Oracles are supposed to warn of impending danger,' he told the animal. 'But I've never heard of them actually being the impending danger they're warning of!'

MODENA
ITALY

Twenty Again

When he turned eighty, Nasrudin threw himself a party.

Amid the huge rumpus of celebrations, the balloons, and good cheer, an enormous tiramisu birthday cake was wheeled out by the wise fool himself.

One of the guests asked why there were only twenty candles on the cake.

'Because,' Nasrudin answered curtly, 'I'm not actually eighty, I'm just twenty for the fourth time!'

HELSINKI
FINLAND

Updated Brain

Nasrudin had been sent by his boss to Finland but he couldn't learn Suomi, the native language.

Despite trying hard, he couldn't grasp even the most elementary grammar or vocabulary.

Weeks passed, and the wise fool remained at the bottom of the class.

Then, one morning, he turned up to the language school and was able to chat away in fluent Finnish, with the accent of a native speaker.

Unable to believe her ears, the teacher asked in bewilderment how the student learned the language overnight.

'Simple,' Nasrudin said, with an ear-to-ear smile. 'I went online after class yesterday and downloaded the latest version of my brain with Suomi pre-installed.'

KABUL
AFGHANISTAN

Power Over Me

At the Afghan capital's famous caged-bird market, Nasrudin spied a frail hoopoe for sale.

Feeling a pang of sorrow for the little creature, he bought it, along with a large bamboo cage.

As soon as he reached the house in which he was staying, he put the cage on a table and spoke to the hoopoe.

'Now I've saved you from the unscrupulous bird dealer who owned you, I'm going to look after you better than any hoopoe has ever been looked after before.'

The bird sat on the floor of the cage, motionless.

The wise fool appeared glum.

'I'm not saying I expected you to jump for joy,' he said, 'but I was hoping you'd tweet in a display of pleasure.'

The little hoopoe continued to sit in silence on the floor of the cage.

Nasrudin sighed.

'I can see you're not satisfied with the lodgings I've provided,' he said. 'Even though I assure you a great many hoopoes live in far smaller cages, I can imagine what trauma you've suffered at the hands of the wretched bird-sellers.'

The little hoopoe just sat there.

Again, the wise fool sighed.

Then, reaching into the cage, he removed the bird and clambered inside himself.

'Don't expect me to always be this generous,' he said. 'But you seem to have a power over me that other birds have not.'

BARCELONA
SPAIN

Most Evil Knife in the World

hile chopping onions at the restaurant where he was employed as a sous chef, Nasrudin cut his thumb badly.

He was furious – not at himself for being careless – but at the knife for injuring him.

'I'm going to make an example of you, you damned knife!' he crowed.

Taking the knife out in front of the restaurant, he put it on a chair, along with a sign that read:

MOST EVIL KNIFE
IN THE WORLD!

The owner of the restaurant came out to see why a crowd was gathering.

'What on earth are you doing?!' he barked at the sous chef. 'Get back in the kitchen where you belong!'

'I'm just getting my own back at the knife that cut me,' Nasrudin snivelled.

The restaurant's owner gave the chef a look of utter consternation.

'Do you really think it cares?'

'No! It plainly doesn't, which is the reason it cut me in the first place!'

BAGHDAD
IRAQ

Empty Threats

asrudin was riding his donkey through the desert west of the Euphrates River.

It was a scorching day, and the poor animal was parched, overloaded, and lame. Despite this, the wise fool was yelling a stream of insults at the creature at the top of his lungs.

'I'm going to beat you until you collapse! Then I'll cut off your ears and use them for slippers! After that I'll chop you up and make sausages of you, and boil your bones down for glue – you damned wretch!'

Just as he was about to bellow another line of insults, an animal rights activist jumped out from behind a thorn-bush.

'How dare you abuse that creature!' he cried.

'But my donkey doesn't mind at all,' Nasrudin replied casually.

'How d'you know she doesn't mind?!'

'She's been with me a very long while.'

'What difference does that make?'

'It means she knows as well as me that they're empty threats.'

UTRECHT
THE NETHERLANDS

Awkward Questions

Nasrudin was singing a lullaby to his wooden clogs, as he did each night before he turned in to bed.

Unknown to him, a thief had crept in through an open window and was tiptoeing through the house in search of loot to steal.

As he crept past the open door to the bedroom, he saw the wise fool sitting on his bed, singing to his clogs.

Forgetting he was an intruder, he asked Nasrudin what he was doing.

The wise fool looked up, frowned, and said:

'I could ask you the same question.'

PRAGUE
CZECH REPUBLIC

Face in the Mirror

Nasrudin had travelled to Prague in the hope of having his portrait painted.

He had heard that the streets of the capital were filled with artists who'd capture his likeness at a bargain basement price.

But, arriving on an autumnal day, fallen leaves blowing through the streets, he realized that the services of even the least expensive painter were way above his means.

As he tramped back to the guesthouse where he was staying, he passed a shop selling discounted picture frames and mirrors.

Pausing there for a moment, he found himself staring at himself in an ornate rococo mirror.

A fraction of the cost of an oil portrait, it was all he had wanted, and yet far more.

Buying it, he hurried back to his room.

He unwrapped it, propped it up against the bed, peered into it, and marvelled at the rendering.

'Such an uncanny likeness!' he gasped. 'Others may say you're only a mirror, but to me you were conjured by the finest artist that ever lived! What other master could depict his subject in such a way that the likeness was updated each day... and at no extra price?!'

Finis

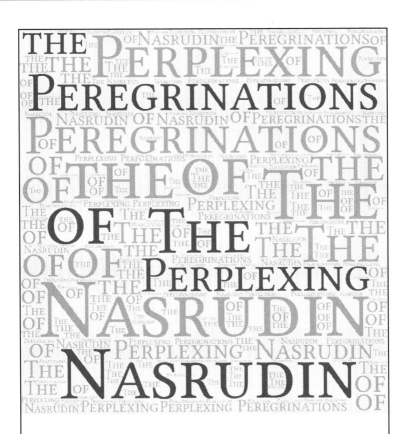

THE
PEREGRINATIONS
OF THE
PERPLEXING
NASRUDIN

TAHIR SHAH

THE VOYAGES AND VICISSITUDES OF NASRUDIN

TAHIR SHAH

TRAVELS WITH NASRUDIN

TAHIR SHAH

A REQUEST

If you enjoyed this book, please review it on your favourite online retailer or review website.

Reviews are an author's best friend.

To stay in touch with Tahir Shah, and to hear about his upcoming releases before anyone else, please sign up for his mailing list:

 http://tahirshah.com/newsletter

And to follow him on social media, please go to any of the following links:

 http://www.twitter.com/humanstew

 @tahirshah999

 http://www.facebook.com/TahirShahAuthor

 http://www.youtube.com/user/tahirshah999

 http://www.pinterest.com/tahirshah

 https://www.goodreads.com/tahirshahauthor

http://www.tahirshah.com

Made in the USA
Middletown, DE
26 July 2021